ORS X

THE MAN WHO KILLED HIMSELF

THE MAN WHO KILLED HIMSELF

Julian Symons

Chivers Press • G.K. Hall & Co.
Bath, England   Thorndike, Maine USA

This Large Print edition is published by Chivers Press, England, and by G.K. Hall & Co., USA.

Published in 1999 in the U.K. by arrangement with the author's estate, care of Curtis Brown.

Published in 1999 in the U.S. by arrangement with Curtis Brown UK.

U.K. Hardcover   ISBN 0–7540–3741-X (Chivers Large Print)
U.K. Softcover   ISBN 0–7540–3742–8 (Camden Large Print)
U.S. Softcover   ISBN 0–7838–8586–5 (Nightingale Series Edition)

The text of this Large Print edition is unabridged.
Other aspects of the book may vary from the original edition.

Set in 16 pt. New Times Roman.

Printed in Great Britain on acid-free paper.

British Library Cataloguing in Publication Data available

Library of Congress Cataloging-in-Publication Data

Symons, Julian, 1912–
       The man who killed himself / Julian Symons.
       p. (large print) cm.
       ISBN 0–7838–8586–5 (lg. print : sc : alk. paper)
       1. Large type books.   I. Title.
       [PR6037.Y5M37   1999]
       823'.912—dc21   99–18824

rdinge

NOTE

My thanks are due to Mr. A. J. Nathan of L. and H. Nathan, the famous court, theatrical and film costumiers, for information about wigs in general, and for taking a benevolent interest in the affairs of Major Easonby Mellon. Readers will be reassured to know that Major Mellon's deception is practicable, and in fact is not unknown in real life.

PART ONE

BEFORE THE ACT

CHAPTER ONE

MR. BROWNJOHN AT HOME

In the end Arthur Brownjohn killed himself, but in the beginning he made up his mind to murder his wife. He did so on the day that Major Easonby Mellon met Patricia Parker. Others might have come to such a decision earlier but Arthur Brownjohn was a patient and, as all those who knew him agreed, a timid and long-suffering man. When people say that a man is long-suffering they mean that they see no reason why he should not suffer for ever.

Major Mellon met Patricia Parker on a Wednesday in April. On the day before that Arthur Brownjohn returned to his home in Fraycut at about five in the afternoon. The house was called The Laurels, although there was no remaining trace of a laurel tree. It was a small square detached house made of red brick, with a neat garden in front and a larger one, just as neat, behind. There are hundreds of such houses in Fraycut, and they are loved by those who live in them because they establish so satisfactorily their owners' position in society. Arthur's wife Clare greeted him with a fierce peck on the cheek and the news that the hedge needed clipping. She was a

3

powerful woman with one of those red healthy faces that carry with them a suggestion of hunting and horse shows. Clare was two inches taller than Arthur, and it might have seemed that she was physically better equipped for hedge clipping than he. It was her expressed belief, however, that it did Arthur good to get out into the air, and now she stood with hands on hips watching him from outside the french window in the drawing-room while he unsteadily climbed a pair of steps and snipped at the hedge.

'Not quite even, a little more off there on the right,' she said and then, like a sergeant-major calling a recruit to attention, 'Arthur. What are those trousers?'

He looked down from the steps. 'Trousers?'

'They are your best gaberdine.'

'Not my *best*.'

She did not relent. 'You know you don't wear them for gardening. Go up and change.'

Arthur had already changed once, from business suit to gaberdine trousers, but he changed again. Clare went into the house.

Clip the hedges, trim the edges, mow the lawn. These were among his duties. It was half past six when he put away the gardening tools in the garage that contained no motor car, and then it was to find that Clare was dressing. Time for him to change again. The Paynes were coming for bridge.

'I should really like to have a bath.'

4

'Can't,' she said. 'I've just had one, water won't be hot. Besides, there's no time.'

The Paynes arrived just before seven-thirty. They were one of half a dozen bridge-playing couples with whom the Brownjohns exchanged visits. The procedure on these occasions varied very little. The visitors had one or perhaps two drinks, a rubber of bridge was played, sandwiches and coffee were served by the hostess, more bridge was played and at some time between eleven and twelve o'clock a good-night whisky was offered. The whole thing made, as Clare said when she won, a thoroughly nice evening.

Mr. Payne was the manager of the Fraycut branch of the bank at which Arthur and Clare had a joint account. He was not, as Clare had often said to her husband, quite out of the top drawer.

'Funny old weather we're having,' he said as he sipped his sherry. 'Rain and shine, rain and shine. April though, I suppose you must expect it. How was it in London?' He spoke as if Fraycut were at the other end of Britain, instead of half an hour's journey from London.

'About the same as here.' Mr. Brownjohn twiddled his glass.

'You can't trust the English weather.' Clare mentioned the weather as if it were an unreliable servant.

'That's just what I always say.' Mrs. Payne said it, as she said everything, with a nervous

5

rush. 'What's the summer going to be like? You can't tell. So George and I are going to Spain.'

'The Costa Brava?' Clare asked with a note of ennui. The Brownjohns never went abroad for holidays, and indeed had not been away together for years.

'The Costa *Blanca*. They say it's nicer, so much less crowded.'

'How odd,' Clare bayed in her deepest tones. 'I was in Penquick's yesterday. The Penquicks are going to Costa Blanca. Perhaps you may see them there.'

There was silence after this remark. The Penquicks owned a grocery shop in the High Street. Mr. Brownjohn offered more sherry, poured it into three glasses. His wife said sharply: 'Arthur.'

'My dear.'

'No more for you. You know you haven't a head for liquor.'

Arthur left his glass unfilled. Mr. Payne and his wife exchanged a meaningful glance. They had heard similar conversations in the past.

'Well,' Mr. Payne said, 'Bring out the devil's playthings. After all, that's what we're here for.'

'I think it's absurd to call them that,' his wife riposted. 'As long as you don't play for high stakes and don't take it too seriously, there's no harm in it.'

Clare made no comment. She played with a

concentration that was terrifying to behold.

Eight, nine, ten, eleven o'clock. Husbands and wives played together, and the Brownjohns held bad cards or had bad luck or played badly. They lost every rubber. The financial deficit was small, the mental irritation extreme. 'What made you double that heart call?' Clare asked her husband. 'Surely anybody with eyes in his head could see that wasn't what I wanted. Just because you're sitting with the king and two others.'

Mr. Payne wagged a finger. 'Now now. No inquests.'

'The trouble is Arthur's not here half the time.' She spoke as if her husband were physically absent. 'I don't know where he is. In cloud-cuckoo-land.'

'Or in the attic,' Mr. Payne said with a loud laugh. 'Racing those cars round the track.' It was a source of amusement to all visitors that Arthur kept a complete layout for model electric car racing up in the attic with a quadruple track, a special Le Mans start, bridges and cross-overs, and twenty different cars.

'We had bad cards, my dear.' Arthur was pouring whisky into cut glass tumblers.

'Give you your revenge next week,' Mr. Payne said. 'Tuesday, Wednesday? The Grevilles are coming over for a game on Monday.'

Arthur coughed. 'I'm afraid I may be away

7

in the middle of next week. Shall we let you know a little later on?'

'You do that,' Mr. Payne said heartily. He finished his whisky. 'Come on, my dear, we've made our fortune, let's go and think how to spend it.'

*   *   *

'I feel so *sorry* for him, George,' Mrs. Payne said as he drove sedately home. 'I mean, it's downright humiliating, telling him not to have another drink.'

'I believe he has got a weak head.'

'I dare say. But she doesn't have to say it like that. He's such a nice little man.'

'Not much meat in those sandwiches.' He negotiated a traffic light. 'You know, she was a Slattery before she married. It makes a difference.'

'I don't see that.'

'She married beneath her,' George Payne said in a tone that denied the possibility of further conversation on the subject.

*   *   *

Back at The Laurels they were stacking plates in the kitchen. There was no need to wash up because Susan, the daily, would do that on the following morning. Arthur interrupted Clare's analysis of his failings during the second rubber.

'My dear.'

'What?'

'I wish you wouldn't say that about my not taking another drink.'

'You know the effect alcohol has on you. Remember the Watsons.'

'That was seven years ago.' But he knew that the occasion, on which he had danced and sung and tried to take off all his clothes, would never be forgotten. He said feebly, 'I'm sure the Paynes thought it odd.'

'The Paynes.' Clare snorted quite loudly, like a horse. 'A jumped-up fellow. In trade.'

'A bank manager is not exactly in trade.'

'As good as. Going to Spain with the grocer.' Abruptly she said, 'What are you doing next week?'

'I shall be away to-morrow. I have to visit Birmingham and Manchester.'

'You're away as much as if you were a commercial traveller.'

'I *am* a sort of commercial traveller. If you want to sell car parts—'

'Spare me the details.' Clare turned away her head. 'I shall go to bed.'

'I'll bring up your drink. Then I shall tidy up.'

The Laurels was a tidy house. In the small square hall there was a square Baluchistan rug, a good rug as Clare often said, which belonged to her family. Above the rug hung a portrait of her father, Mr. Slattery, a square-jawed man with large square nostrils. He stared across at the opposite wall with fierce contemptuous eyes. The sitting-room led to the left off the hall. It contained a sofa and two matching arm-chairs with loose covers, set at precisely the proper angles to each other. A glass-fronted cabinet was filled with books, most of them inherited from the Slattery connection. Little Victorian tables were dotted about and room had been found for a television set, which Clare moved about frequently because she felt that really it did not belong. Victorian ornaments stood on the mantelpiece, together with an old photograph of the Slattery family in Calcutta, Mr. Slattery with arms folded, his wife wispy in something loose, Clare holding a tennis racket. The dining-room was on the right of the hall. Six chairs sat in it round a gate-leg table and beside one wall stood a twin cabinet to the one in the sitting-room containing the best china used only for visitors. More utilitarian crockery hung from the kitchen dresser. In the kitchen larder various spots were labelled 'Jams,' 'Cereals,' 'Tea,' because Susan constantly put things away in the wrong places. A plastic chart with differently-coloured pegs reminded Clare what to buy and when to buy it.

Arthur made Clare the drink of hot whisky and lime which she invariably had as a nightcap, and took it up to where she sat

10

waiting in her single bed, face creamed and hair in a net. They had played bridge in the sitting-room, which did not look as it should have done. Arthur put away the card table, returned chairs to their places, plumped up cushions. Then he went up past the bedroom to the attic. This large windowless coved room (a window would have disturbed the outside symmetry of the house) ran almost the whole length of the house. Half of it was occupied by the slot racing layout, the tracks bending in a double eight with two exciting chicane sections where cars could really go all out. Spectator stands with people in them, car pits with engineers waiting for cars to come in, television camera crews, hay bales, banking at bends, were all in place. Four cars stood ready to start. He thought of racing them, but knew that the sound would keep Clare awake. The other half of the attic contained much china discarded from down below, framed water colours painted by his mother when he had been a child, and his old roll-topped desk. He unlocked this with a key from the ring at his waist. A loose leaf book in a black cover lay on the desk. It was his diary.

The first page said: 'A. Brownjohn, The Laurels, Fraycut, Surrey, England, Europe, The World.' Below there was a little rhyme which he had once read and repeated, perhaps inaccurately:

He who unbidden looks within
Commits a fearful wicked sin.
Peeping Tom, filthy fool,
I bet you were a sneak at school.

He opened the diary, read one or two of the entries, ran his fingers over an untouched white page, decided that he was too tired to write and locked the desk again.

In the bathroom he paused while brushing his teeth to consider the face that confronted him. It was pale, thin-lipped, distinctly rabbitish round the nose and doggy about the eyes. Worst of all was the billiard-ball smoothness of the head. Arthur had started losing his hair at an early age, and by the time he was in his early thirties the whole lot had gone. He had once seen Yul Brynner on the screen and had tried to convince himself that baldness was attractive, but examination of his head in the glass had made it clear that the total effect produced by his features did not at all resemble that of Yul Brynner's.

He went into the bedroom. Clare was lying as he had known she would be, on her right side with her eyes half closed. Her face was covered with shiny cream. He kissed the top of her head, undressed and got into bed, turned out the light. In the darkness he repeated what he had said earlier. 'I wish you wouldn't say that about my drinking. I don't like it.'

She made no reply. Five minutes later she

began to snore.

CHAPTER TWO

THE AFFAIRS OF MAJOR EASONBY MELLON

On the following day Major Easonby Mellon turned into one of the side streets on the good—that is to say the Hanover Square—side of Regent Street, walked into an office block named Romany House and took the lift to the second floor. He used a key to open a door that said in black lettering 'Matrimonial Assistance Limited, Major Easonby Mellon,' and stepped inside. He was at once ankle deep in letters, a delicious sensation. He picked up the armful of letters and went into his office, which had a window looking out on to the street. There was a large chair behind his handsome desk, and a couple of other chairs for clients. Opposite to his desk stood a filing cabinet and also another smaller desk with a covered typewriter on it. Visitors assumed what seemed obvious, that this desk was used by Major Mellon's secretary, but the assumption was wrong for the Major had no secretary.

Major Mellon took off his pork pie hat, sat at his desk humming like a bumble bee and opened the post with a neat letter opener. There were nearly seventy letters, and some half of them contained cheques or postal orders. He was a dapper little figure as he sat behind the desk, occasionally whistling a little at what he read, for people write odd things to matrimonial agencies. He wore a suit in a dog tooth check that was perhaps a little loud, gay socks, and well-polished brown shoes. His tie and shirt were reasonably sober, he had a good thatch of brownish hair with a tinge of red in it, and a neat beard. When he had read the post he carefully put all the cheques and postal orders into a drawer, separated the first applications from the follow-ups and went across to his filing cabinet.

Matrimonial Assistance Limited operated in a manner similar to that of some other, although not the largest and most reputable, matrimonial agencies. The Major advertised in local newspapers and on dozens of newsagents' boards. His correspondents received an encouraging letter saying that there were hundreds of bachelors, spinsters, widowers and widows on his books. A small remittance would bring the correspondent a list of a dozen names of ladies (or gentlemen, as the case might be) who wished, in the words of the duplicated letter, to assume 'the sweet bonds of matrimony.' The brief descriptions did not include addresses because, as the letter explained, it was a fixed rule that all

14

introductions must be handled through Matrimonial Assistance. 'This is our pleasure and your safeguard,' the letter said. Letters came in and were forwarded, correspondents eventually met in the office (by appointment only, for the Major was not there every day), and marriages no doubt took place. It was not Major Mellon's part, as he had sometimes to say firmly, to examine the antecedents of people who wrote to him. He credited them all with honesty and common sense, and if some were lacking in one or other of these qualities that was hardly Major Mellon's business.

He looked at his diary and saw that he had only two appointments, one at eleven-thirty, the other half an hour later. There was time to do some typing. The first applications received his duplicated letter, signed 'Easonby Mellon' with 'Major, R.A.C. (retd.)' beneath. Major Mellon signed these letters dashingly, with his left hand. Then came the follow-ups, from people who had responded to the duplicate letter and sent remittances. They got their list of names taken from the files with a request that they should not write to more than one name on the list at a time—although, of course, this request was not always obeyed. That left four letters needing more personal attention. He skimmed through one of them, in a woman's hand:

' ... seemed a perfect gentleman, or otherwise as you can imagine I should never have invited him into my home, but as soon as he was inside he began to behave like a wild beast, I feel sure that you . . .'

How foolish people were! He chuckled a little at the thought of it. The man described himself on his record card as 'Poultry breeder (55) of loving disposition,' and he lived in Norfolk. The Major reflected that he would have to write to the fellow seriously, and of course he must send a sympathetic note to the lady ('Widow, petite, early 40s but attractive'), something about her fatal charm perhaps? It was now, however, time for his eleven-thirty visitors.

These proved to be a Mr. Lake, a gangling Australian with a terrible squint, and a nervous ageing spinster named Amelia Bonnamie. Could that really be her name? But there again, what she chose to call herself was not his concern. He said that his secretary had just gone out, expanded on it a little ('To tell the truth I asked her to step out for a few minutes, thought it might be easier for everybody') and talked briefly about the sacred bond of matrimony. They seemed pleased, with him and with each other. As they were going he tapped Lake on the shoulder.

'Just a moment.' He closed the door on Miss Bonnamie, leaving her in the tiny outer hall. 'When an introduction is effected a small fee is payable by the gentleman. Three guineas.'

'Of course. Sorry I forgot.' The Australian

16

almost fell over himself in his eagerness to get out the money.

The Major took it, gave him a receipt and said with what might have been a twinkle in his eye, 'I hope your intentions are serious.'

'You bet,' said Lake, and was gone. It was a nicely ambiguous reply.

The other appointment—well, the Major drew down the corners of his mouth as he thought of that, and re-read the letter on his desk signed in a neat hand 'Patricia Parker (Miss).' The letter said that the writer was in her middle twenties—add ten years on to *that*, the Major thought—and unattached, and that she wished to meet a gentleman rather older than herself with marriage in mind. Miss Parker said that she had been a secretary, but was not working at the moment. She wrote from an address in one of London's northern suburbs. In the last paragraph she wrote in her neat, rather characterless hand: 'I understand the usual thing is to put applicants in touch by letter, but before deciding whether I wish to avail myself of this service I should be glad if I might see you personally, as there are certain points I would like to discuss with you.'

Something about the stilted phrases had caught the Major's attention. He knew from past experience that the point for discussion would probably be the revelation that Miss Parker had an old mother who would be expected to share the home of the married pair, or was handicapped in her search for a husband by a wooden leg, or wanted to put before him some other mental or physical problem that, so far as he was concerned, was insoluble. It was unwise to see her, no doubt about it. Yet there had been occasions in the past when such letters from women clients had led to delicious little romances of a personal kind. There was something about this letter, although he could not have said what, that made him answer it. Now, as he re-read the letter and waited for Miss Parker, he told himself that he had been foolish. It was obvious that she was one of the wooden leg brigade.

'Half an hour,' the Major said aloud—he often talked to himself when he was alone. 'Half an hour with Miss Pegleg and then a spot of lunch.' And after lunch he would pay in the cash to the bank, an occupation which always gave him pleasure. The outer bell rang. He went outside, ushered in Miss Parker, asked her to sit down. As she sat opposite him, demure and not quite smiling, Major Mellon took a good look at her and was frankly bowled over.

Patricia Parker did not look a day over twenty-five. Her face was pretty rather than characterful, but pretty it undoubtedly was. She had a beautiful skin, her brown hair shone silkily, her figure—well, it was not easy to judge when she sat in a chair but she was obviously shapely, and it was just as obvious that neither of the legs she displayed to him was a wooden one. Miss Parker was no dazzling beauty but she was a pretty young woman, and pretty young women did not often come Major Mellon's way in the course of business. For a moment or two he goggled at her. Then he recovered.

'My dear Miss Parker,' he leaned forward conspiratorially. 'I have sent my secretary out for half an hour. Unfortunately these offices are not as spacious as I could wish, and I thought that perhaps you had something confidential to discuss . . .'

He left the sentence unfinished. Miss Parker said that was thoughtful of him. Her voice was low, pleasant, unemphatic.

'You wanted to have a chat with me in person. Here I am.'

'Yes.' She seemed to find it hard to know how to begin, and Major Mellon continued. Suspicion had quickly replaced pleasure in his mind. Was this girl trying to play a trick on him? His next words were spoken bluntly, almost harshly.

'Forgive me for saying so, but it surprises me that you should have any difficulty in finding a husband. I am here to help, but I doubt if there is anything Matrimonial Assistance can do for you that you couldn't do quite easily yourself.'

'Don't say that.' It was the first sign of

19

emotion she had shown. 'Please don't say that.'

The Major softened, but only slightly, and suggested that she should tell him about it.

'It's difficult. I don't know if I can.'

'Try.'

'I can't if you're looking at me. Will you close your eyes—or look out of the window. Then I might be able to.'

So Major Mellon swung round his chair, turned his back on her and looked at the people passing below in the street while he heard the story Patricia Parker told in her even voice. It was not, after all, such a very unusual story. Her name at birth was not Patricia Parker but Hildegarde Sommer. She was a German, and had been living in Germany with her mother—her father had been killed on the Eastern front—when the Russians swept in. As a child of five she had seen her mother raped by half a dozen Russian soldiers. Afterwards her mother had committed suicide. Hildegarde had been placed in a camp, and had come to England when she was in her teens to do housework. When she was twenty-one she had married a man named Parker, with whom she had been going out for some time. A week after their marriage he had asked her to do certain awful things—she did not specify their nature—and she had left him and later got a divorce. She had qualified as a secretary and could earn her living, but she did not feel it was enough to earn a living. She wanted to be married, and had gone out with several men. 'But it was no good, you understand? Yet I feel that I wish to be married, I could make a good wife for a man who was kind, a man perhaps older than myself, do you understand?'

'Can I turn round now?'

'Yes. Thank you for listening to me.'

He turned. She was staring at him as though he were an oracle. Was the story true or not? Upon the whole he thought that some of it was true and some invented, but it did not seem to him that this mattered very much.

'Do you think you will be able to help me?' she asked solemnly.

The Major got up, came round the desk, and lifted one of the pretty hands that were crossed in her lap. She allowed it to stay in his hand and sat looking up at him.

'I know what an effort it must have been to tell me that, Patricia—I may call you that, I hope, my dear? And if we can help you we shall. But I tell you what we're going to do first of all. We're going out together to have a spot of lunch at a little place round the corner, just the two of us. If I'm to help I shall have to know a little more about the sort of person you are. That is, if you're free for lunch.'

'I have no other engagement.' Major Mellon was delighted with the simplicity and candour of her reply.

As he was closing the door she remarked, 'Your secretary has not come back.'

The Major rode that one easily. 'She has her own key.'

The little place round the corner was also an expensive place, the spot of lunch included lobster thermidor and a bottle of excellent white burgundy. Pat—by the time that lunch was over he was calling her Pat—viewed it all with open-eyed wonder. She loved the alcove in which they sat, where the Major's hand occasionally and as if by chance touched hers, she exclaimed upon the excellence of the service, she wondered at her host's expertise in ordering the wine. Did a warning sense tell Major Mellon that there was something not quite right, not quite real, about Patricia Parker's childlike delight at being taken out to lunch? Perhaps, but it seemed that any game she might be up to could not possibly affect him. And in any case he was charmed, scenting as he did a delicious little romance. When they parted it was with the assurance that she would come to the office again to-morrow, by which time he would have thought over the problem further, and might be able to suggest some correspondents who could be recommended as potential husbands.

Major Easonby Mellon returned to the office in a daze of pleasure. He had three more interviews with couples during the afternoon which he handled rather absent-mindedly. At half past five he closed the office and went home.

Home was Number 48 Elm Drive, Clapham, a street of solid grey Victorian houses leading off Clapham Common's south side, which had so far escaped the maw of the developer. The Major and his wife had the upper part of the house, which was divided into two. When he opened the door he smelled cooking, a smell strong, spicy and not at all disagreeable. Joan was in the kitchen and Major Mellon crept up behind her and put his arms round her plump waist. She gave a delighted scream.

'E. Supper's not ready. I didn't expect you yet.'

'But here I am,' the Major said gaily. 'And very very hungry.'

'You'll have to wait.'

'That's not what I'm hungry for.' He stroked his little beard. 'I am a traveller in a desert who has just reached the longed-for oasis.'

'Don't be silly. I've got supper to look after, it will spoil. E, whatever are you doing? Put me down.'

The Major, who had begun to carry her from the kitchen to the sitting-room, complied, for he was a small man and Joan was a fair weight. In the sitting-room he took her on his knee. 'And what has my little lady been doing while I've been away?'

'Oh, nothing. It's what *you've* been doing that's interesting. I think women have an awful time.'

'Men must work and women must weep.'

23

He made an adroit move, and Joan found herself beneath him on the sofa. She protested.

'Stop it, E, I said supper will spoil, there really isn't time. Oh, not here please, let's go into the bedroom at least.'

'Here,' said Major Easonby Mellon firmly. And there it was. It was enjoyable, and would have been more enjoyable still if the image of Patricia Parker (Miss) had not remained so persistently in his mind. Afterwards Joan sighed.

'Trouble is I don't feel like getting supper now. Shall we just go to bed?'

'Certainly not. The labourer is worthy of his hire.'

While they had supper she said, 'Come on, what have you been doing? Tell me some of the things that have been happening, the way you always do.'

In a way Joan was not unlike Pat, he reflected, the same sort of round face and almost the same shade of brown hair. And Joan, of course, had very good legs. But the likeness only showed how unwise it was to let yourself go to seed as Joan had done, because there could be no comparison in their attractiveness. Mark you, Joan was thirty-five, or was it thirty-six? But she could never have been in quite the same class as Pat . . .

'What's been *happening*, I asked you.' Joan's voice had a note of querulousness, and the

Major brought himself back to matters in hand.

'Let me see, now. Friday—on Friday the chief sent for me and said the job in Norway had fizzled out. Our chap over there, Bjornson, had been selling stuff to the Russians all the time, and this story about a new rocket device was just a plant he was trying on us.'

'He was trying to trick you? To get you sent out there so that they could kill you?'

'Oh, I don't suppose so. Just trying to mislead us, you know, both sides are doing it all the time.'

'And what have you done about him, this man, Johnson?'

'Bjornson. Nothing much. I believe the chief's making a higher bid for his services. We want him to go on working for the Russians, naturally, that's the chief's whole idea.' The Major was familiar with the work of Mr. John le Carré and Mr. Deighton, and moved easily in this world of the triple- and quadruple-cross. In the manner of the masters he added, 'Spying's a dirty business.'

He embroidered the theme. It had long ceased to be a matter of surprise to him that Joan accepted his inventions so readily. The first step, by which he convinced her that he was an agent, had been the big one. With that surmounted, why should she not believe the tales he told her about the dingy office in Soho and the erratic-tempered chief, the internecine warfare between the rival Department AX 15 and his own UGLI 3 which as he often complained occupied the greater part of their time, the troubles with men in the field and his own occasional trips abroad to rebuke one agent or bribe another, the very infrequent spurts of violence? He congratulated himself sometimes on the fact that he never pitched the stories too steep, so that there were no incidents which moved beyond his powers of invention or which seemed too outrageously unlikely. The struggles between the Chief and Birkett, who was the head of AX 15, were rather like those of a television serial in which different characters come out on top in successive weeks, and at one time Joan had got bored with them as a viewer gets bored with the repetitious activities of a favourite television character. To-night she gave up after five minutes, and they went to bed.

'Shall I tell you something, E?' she asked, and went on to do so. 'I don't know you, do I? Not the real you. Perhaps the real you is a different person altogether from the one I know.'

He protested vigorously, but as she drifted into sleep it struck him that the phrase about being a different person embodied a truth, although she did not know it. Remove Major Easonby Mellon's good thatch of hair to reveal an egg-bald scalp, take away his beard to show a weak chin, slip out the contact lenses which changed the colour of his eyes from brown to blue, replace the dog tooth check with a suit of indeterminate grey, put him down in Livingstone Road, Fraycut, and he would have been recognised by everybody as Arthur Brownjohn.

Lying beside Joan, who within a few minutes had flung out an arm and like Clare in distant Fraycut begun to snore, Major Easonby Mellon thought of Pat, then Joan, then Clare. There could be no doubt that two women and two lives presented a problem, especially when a man was really interested in a third. And then, as naturally as a coin drops into its appointed slot, it occurred to him that this problem would be solved if Clare did not exist, and that it must surely be possible for a man of his ingenuity to bring about that desirable state of affairs. A life without Clare! The prospect was almost too heady to contemplate. Contemplating it, he fell asleep.

CHAPTER THREE

BACKGROUND OF A DECEPTION

Arthur Brownjohn had always been of an inventive turn of mind, and when the war ended he joined with a man in his regiment named Maser in the purchase of a firm called Lektrek Electricals. Arthur's share of the necessary capital had been provided by his army gratuity, together with a small inheritance he had received from an uncle. Lektreks was a flourishing little firm of electrical contractors, and the partners expected it to provide a living for them while they developed the Brownjohn Patent Clutch. This was a type of automatic clutch that had been invented by Arthur during his long periods of idleness as a sergeant in the Catering Corps. He had demonstrated it to Maser on a number of toy battery-operated motor cars, and he was certain that with a reasonably well-equipped workshop he would be able to make a prototype. The construction of this prototype, however, proved more complicated than he had expected. Months passed before it was perfected, or almost perfect, and then the blow fell. A very similar device was put on the market by one of the big car manufacturers, a device so similar that there was no question of going ahead with the Brownjohn Patent Clutch. A few weeks later Maser disappeared, and Arthur discovered that his partner had been fiddling the books by the simple process of having cheques for some accounts made payable to himself instead of to the firm.

Arthur was reluctant to close down Lektreks, for he had half a dozen other ideas in his mind for which an electrical firm would provide ideal backing—an everlasting torch with a battery which recharged itself automatically, an electrical shock cure for hay fever, an electrified rocking chair, and a vibro pad that would open the pores far better than any cream. At the same time it was obvious that the firm would not provide him with a living unless he gave to it the time that he devoted to his blueprints and experiments. Arthur saw that what he needed was, quite simply, money, but where was it to come from? He had a painful interview with his widower father, a retired customs and excise official who refused to lend him a penny and advised him to do a steady job of work. That avenue was closed, and he had no other approachable relatives. It was at this point that, like many men before him, he realised the immense usefulness of a rich wife.

Arthur's contacts with women had been slight and few, and although he had a strong fantasy life it was not associated with girls. In adolescence he became a surprisingly good tennis player and won the championship of the local club two years in succession. The champion of a tennis club, particularly if he is young and unmarried, is a desirable object to many of the women members, and Arthur had plenty of opportunities for what in such clubs is still euphemistically called flirtation. At this time, however, he rather resembled the man who maintained that if the concept of love had not been invented people would never have experienced the state itself. He was timid, even fearful, in the presence of women, and had had sexual intercourse only once before entering the army. On this occasion he was playing for the tennis team in an away match, and one of the ladies' doubles pair took him home and seduced him in the back of her car. In the army his sexual experiences were more frequent, but equally brief and unsatisfactory. It is not surprising that when Arthur contemplated marriage he went to a matrimonial agency. He soon saw that he had been mistaken in thinking that he was likely to acquire a rich wife by this means, but the set-up of such agencies engaged his mind. Obviously an agency needed very little capital. Might it not be possible to make money out of it? A few weeks later his agency, Marriage For All, was born.

It is hard to say what might have become of Arthur if he had not one day met a friend from his old tennis club, been persuaded to rejoin, and been partnered in a mixed doubles by a meatily handsome woman named Clare Slattery. They found that they made a good doubles pair, and although Arthur was too much out of practice to do well in the singles, they reached the final of the mixed doubles. When Clare had hit a forehand into the net to lose the final she shook Arthur's hand

30

vigorously and said: 'Damned bad shot, partner, I'm sorry. Come and have a drink.'

They had two or three drinks, and under questioning from Clare, Arthur found himself telling her what he did. Marriage For All was already showing signs of being profitable, but Arthur kept this activity a close secret because of its faint absurdity. Instead he talked about his inventions, in particular about an idea he had for driving cars by a series of belts and pulleys which would dispense with the need for gears. Clare listened patiently, although with obvious scepticism.

'Very clever. Be a long time before you make any money out of it, though.'

'Oh, I don't know. It's just a matter of getting going.'

'Not relying on it, I hope?'

Arthur laughed. He had a pleasant laugh, and although his hair was rapidly thinning he was still an engaging young man rather than a rabbity middle-aged one. 'Of course not. It's just a sideline for my firm. I put a couple of men on it from time to time, under my supervision naturally.'

'Not your main source of income?'

'Oh no. We're importers of car spares. We can undercut most British manufacturers by thirty per cent.' In saying this he was telling part of the truth. When he and Maser had bought Lektreks there had indeed been a flourishing business in the importation of cheap spares. Neglect of it, coupled with the defalcations of Maser, had led to the loss of most of their agencies. The small workshop in Bermondsey had been sold and the staff dismissed, and Lektreks now operated from one room in an office block called Paget House, filling orders sent in by long-established clients. With what was for him considerable boldness Arthur asked, 'What kind of job do you do?'

Clare gave one of her gusty laughs. 'Just a bit of part time work for the WVS. I'm independent.'

There was a pause. Then Arthur suggested that they should have another drink.

During the next few weeks they played a great deal of tennis together, and Arthur made some tactful inquiries about Clare. The results were encouraging. Her father had been a fairly important administrator in the Indian Civil Service. Clare had gone to school in England but spent the holidays out in Calcutta, and after leaving school had gone there to live. When her father retired, just before the war, he had bought a house called The Laurels in Fraycut, a prosperous little town in Surrey. Arthur's lodgings were at Stonehead, the next station up the line and a mile or two away, and he fully realised that Fraycut was one social step up from Stonehead. Rich commuters had built houses that were almost small estates on the edge of the town, and he spent an interesting afternoon looking round the place. Livingstone Road was not on this high income commuter level—in another place it might have been called suburban—but still, when he made an exterior inspection of The Laurels, he was impressed by the good bourgeois solidity of the house. Mr. Slattery had been dead for a couple of years, his wife had predeceased him, and there were no other children. Altogether, Clare must be quite comfortably off. She was an attractive proposition, and the attraction was if anything increased by the fact that there was, as he put it to himself, no nonsense about her. Something about the sturdiness of her legs and the rough, slightly chapped nature of her skin seemed to put nonsense quite (to use a tennis term) out of court. After one rather gay evening at the club he proposed, standing with her just outside the club-house. He was faintly disturbed by the alacrity with which he was accepted. It was rather as if he had put his head inside the jaws of an apparently stuffed alligator and had found them decisively snapped together.

They were married at a registry office, and given a good send off by the tennis club members. His father met the bride for the first time on the wedding day, and expressed his opinion of her briefly. 'You won't get much change out of *her*, in bed or out of it,' he said. Clare had mentioned more than once that the rest of the family would be coming to the wedding and that she didn't know what they would think about it, and at the reception Arthur first really became aware of the Slattery connection, in the form of two immensely old men called by Clare Uncle Pugs and Uncle Ratty. Uncle Pugs, whose name was Sir Pelham Slattery, made a short but still rather incoherent speech about Clare being a sweet little girl who had grown up to be a lovely young woman. There was a drop on the end of his nose and Arthur waited for it to fall off. Instead tears from his eyes coursed down his cheeks as he was heard to say, 'Wish every happiness . . . and all the best of . . . ship never . . . rocks . . . Mr. and Mrs. Browning.' He sat down with the drop on his nose still there. It did not seem worth correcting his error.

A little later Uncle Ratty cornered Arthur. Redfaced and apparently in a state of permanent anger, he was a more formidable proposition than Uncle Pugs. His first words were, 'Now you've got her I hope you can keep her.'

'Keep her?' Arthur had a vision of Clare as some great furry animal escaping from him across fields.

'Look after her, man. Pay the bills.'

Arthur goggled. The idea was quite the reverse of that with which he had married, but he realised that this must not be admitted. 'I have my own business.'

'So Clare said. Selling bits of cars or something. Doesn't sound like much to me.'

'We have agencies.'

Uncle Ratty stared hard at him, and it occurred to Arthur that this terrifying specimen of prehistoric man from the Lincolnshire fens probably did not know what an agency was. All he said, however, was, 'Stand on your own feet. Like cattle.'

That was what it sounded like, but Arthur thought that he must have been mistaken. 'I beg your pardon?'

'Thought it would have been plain enough,' Uncle Ratty said, and moved away.

Arthur never discovered what he had said, nor did Uncle Pugs and Uncle Ratty appear again during his married life. They sank back into the fens from which they had emerged, communicating only by means of cards at Christmas. It was not, however, the last he heard of the Slattery connection, for it was made plain to him that the reception had been a crucial test which he had failed. He later discovered that Uncle Pugs and Uncle Ratty were distant cousins and not real uncles at all, and that in fact Clare had no close relations, but that did not affect their plain perception that he was not up to the mark. It often occurred to Arthur in later years to wonder why Clare had married him. He came to the conclusion that the idea of marrying somebody socially beneath her was really positively congenial, although she pretended otherwise. To social inferiority was added Arthur's natural timidity, which made it easy for her to overbear him on any point, and when these qualities were topped by his disinclination for nonsense he became (as he saw afterwards) an almost ideal husband. Even the failure of the Slattery connection had its compensations so far as Clare was concerned, for it provided permanent proof both of her superiority to her husband and of the sacrifice she had made for him.

The many respects in which he found her less than an ideal wife are too obvious to need cataloguing, but one must be mentioned specifically. So far from marrying a wife happy to provide financial backing that would make it possible for him to give all his time to research, Arthur found that Clare kept her private income intact, and expected him to give her a fixed sum each week for housekeeping. Certainly he lived rent free at The Laurels, certainly also Clare was an economical housekeeper, with a liking for salads and rather sparse vegetarian dishes, but he speedily found the untruth of the old saying that two can live as cheaply as one. The truth was, as he acknowledged in his diary, that he had not grasped the realities of marriage. He had been looking for a bank account, Clare had been looking for a necessary social appendage, and she had got much the better of the bargain. Indeed, her life changed very little from what it had been when she was single. She had a number of regular commitments, which included an afternoon a week at the local Liberal Party offices, one morning a fortnight on a Children's Care Committee, and a visit to Weybridge every Wednesday to shop and attend an art class. She took up other occupations from time to time, including prison visiting, Oxfam and the W.V.S. work which she had mentioned to him, but these were abandoned for one reason or another. Her only problem was that of fitting a husband into the busy round. There was also the tennis club, but the charms of that faded for both of them soon after marriage. And there were social occasions on which a husband was undoubtedly useful, little evenings at home sometimes associated with the Liberal Party but more often with bridge, which both of them played. Arthur's life was a blend of such evenings with gardening and the variety of duties that Clare found for him about the house. It was from the emotional pressures of such a life, and the financial pressure of having to pay for it, that Major Easonby Mellon was born.

Perhaps Arthur did not know himself what he meant to do with the Marriage For All Bureau after his marriage, but it was soon clear to him that it or some similar business would have to be continued, since it was his only considerable source of income. Marriage For All had the disadvantage that he was connected with it in his own person and under his own name. Supposing that he started another agency of a similar kind but run by a different person? Acting was one of the few spheres in which he had shone at school, and he had always taken an obscure pleasure in dressing up.

The idea presented several problems, but they were of a kind that Arthur took pleasure in solving. The name of Easonby Mellon, derived partly from the financier Andrew Mellon and partly from the hero of a book he had enjoyed as a schoolboy, was the least of them. The military rank seemed appropriate and the clothes, wig and beard were designed as suitable to it. The wig maker he went to appreciated the interest shown by his client. He was surprised when Arthur said that he did not want to match his original faded light brown colouring, but he asked no questions. Arthur had been keen on a red wig, which he felt would express Easonby Mellon's personality, but he had been persuaded that a brown one with reddish tints would be far less conspicuous.

'The usual problem of course, sir, is matching the natural hair colour at back and sides, but in your case—' The wig maker coughed, and it was true that Arthur was quite remarkably lacking in hair.

The wig was thick and curly and he was delighted by the fact that he could comb it so that (as he was shown with mirrors) perfectly genuine scalp would show through the invisible net foundation. 'Nobody would know,' he said exultantly.

The wig maker, who had himself a splendid head of hair, was solemn. 'Nobody at all, sir. I know husbands whose wives have no idea that they wear a wig.'

'Is that really so? Even when—'

'Even then, sir, certainly. And if I may suggest a small but possibly useful refinement—'

'Indeed you may.'

'It may be an advantage to have a trio, showing various stages of development.' Arthur was baffled. The wig maker explained that he could have three wigs, Number One showing the hair cut rather short, Number Two of normal cut, and Number Three with hair growing rather long at the back of the neck. 'I have a client whose wife tells him that he really must go to the barber when he is wearing Number Three. It positively makes his day, sir.'

'I'm sure it does.' He ordered Numbers One, Two and Three accordingly. The wig maker was less enthusiastic about the idea of a beard, saying that this would need great care when eating and shaving, in case it got wet and lost its shape. It seemed to Arthur, however, that a beard was an essential part of Easonby Mellon's personality, and by having it cut well away from the mouth he managed to deal with it successfully.

He was delighted with the result. 'You are an artist,' he said to the wig maker, a wizened, aged figure who perhaps proved his artistic nature by going out of business shortly after executing Arthur's commission, and dying in poverty a few months later. A six line obituary appeared in *The Times*, referring to him as 'a character of the theatrical world.'

There was also the matter of renting an office and of opening a bank account. His first office was down a dingy side street but when a room in the Romany House block fell vacant he took it, signing the lease with his left hand and giving as reference Mr. Brownjohn of Lektreks, who duly sent a letter certifying Major Mellon's reliability as a tenant. He used his left hand also when providing a signature for the bank. It was Arthur Brownjohn, bald, rabbity and darkly suited, who left The Laurels each morning. In the Lektreks office he kept Easonby Mellon's clothes, and he installed a mirror by the help of which, at first with infinite care and some difficulty, he fitted wig and beard. A perfect fitting took nearly half an hour, although under stress he could manage in fifteen minutes. After changing he went down in the self-operating lift and walked to Romany House, which was only a couple of streets and five minutes' walk away.

At first this double identity was a game, a way of safeguarding the shameful secret represented by the fact that his income came from a matrimonial agency, but such games have a way of developing their own meanings and subtleties, so that although we begin by playing them self-indulgently they end by taking charge of us and revealing unexpected facets of our personalities. As months changed into years, and Matrimonial Assistance flourished, and the deception remained immune from detection, its author found a positive pleasure in accentuating his own meekness and timidity at The Laurels in a way which gave additional zest to the exhibition of the very different characteristics of Major Easonby Mellon. There is no difference, Congreve observed, between continued affectation and reality, and Major Mellon proved to Arthur Brownjohn the truth of this aphorism. He was self-assured where Arthur was hesitant, brusque where he was compliant, an eager eater and drinker where Arthur was a frugal one. That is, Major Mellon became all of these things by pleasant experimentation. He developed also a quite unArthurian liking for a bit of nonsense, first made manifest when a woman aspirant to marriage began to take off her clothes in the office one day, and the Major found himself eagerly helping her.

Joan was the most notable of several bits of

nonsense. She had turned up one day after writing a letter, a good-natured plump woman in her late twenties, whose husband had been killed in Korea. On that first afternoon she had succumbed to the Major's advances, and thereafter he took her to a hotel every weekday for a fortnight. It was the sort of situation that had to be resolved in one way or another partly because Joan, although rather vague, had realised that the matrimonial agency did not occupy the whole of his time, partly because he felt an urgent need for some relief from Clare. Marriage was the answer, marriage and the setting up of a second, quite distinct home for his second personality. Arthur Brownjohn was terrified by the idea, but Major Easonby Mellon carried it through joyfully.

He explained to Joan that his status as a member of UGLI 3 was supposed to preclude marriage, but that for her sake he was prepared to risk it so long as the ceremony was kept absolutely quiet. They signed the register at Caxton Hall in the presence of witnesses brought in from the street, Joan found and rented the apartment in Clapham, and Major Mellon transferred his effects to it. These chiefly consisted of clothes, and Joan exclaimed in wonder at the quality of his suits. Arthur Brownjohn bought his clothes ready made, but Easonby Mellon's tweeds came from Corefinch and Burleigh just off Savile

Row, one of the most expensive tailors in London. Clare had always been incurious about Arthur's business, and when he said that he would have to be away very often in the middle of the week because he was taking over the work of their Midlands and Northern representatives her reaction was simply one of alarm that business might be falling off. Reassured on this point she adapted herself with only occasional grumbles to the absences from home necessitated by his additional work.

So a new pattern of life was fixed for him. From Friday to Monday Arthur Brownjohn was to be found at The Laurels, from Tuesday to Thursday Major Easonby Mellon put up his slippered feet on the sofa at Elm Drive. The wig and beard proved to be the triumphant success that had been predicted. He shaved each morning with an electric razor, and washed only cursorily, taking care to keep water away from the beard. Even in the greatest ardours of their married life Joan did not suspect his secret. Occasionally he varied the pattern of his weekly activities a little, but not very much, for he felt in it a symmetry like that in a work of art. At times he really did make a tour of Birmingham, Manchester, Leeds and other cities in which Lektreks still had customers. And if Joan, that perpetually amiable and resilient cushion, was an almost perfect partner for the part of his nature represented by Major Easonby Mellon, there could be no doubt that Arthur Brownjohn had a basic desire to be dominated by some Clare-like figure. To possess and be possessed by both was almost perfect, or seemed so until the advent of Patricia Parker, which had been preceded early in March by the disastrous affair of Mr. Clennery Tubbs.

CHAPTER FOUR

WYPITKLERE

Clennery Tubbs had appeared on the day that Arthur went to demonstrate a simplified automatic dishwasher of his own invention to a firm named Inter Commerce. This was something on which he had worked intermittently for some years, and it had at one time been in the kitchen at The Laurels. Often it worked perfectly, but upon occasions a destructive gremlin seemed to occupy the washer. The gremlin wrecked this demonstration, at which the activating rods got quite out of hand and broke half the plates. Arthur had been sadly packing it up afterwards, and was on his way out when he was stopped by a small man with wild sandy hair and markedly protruding eyes.

'Rotten luck. Bet it works nine times out of

44

ten.'

'You weren't at the demo, were you?'

'Couldn't help hearing what Jenner was saying.'

'You're quite right. If only they'd give me another trial after I've ironed out that little trouble.'

The man shook his head. 'No good. Won't do it.'

'Certainly Mr. Jenner seemed rather abrupt.' Jenner was the chief engineer of the company, and he had been caustic.

'Jenner's a pig. Won't even touch my invention.'

'Good heavens. And you're part of the firm.'

The man held out a hand. 'Way it goes. Name's Tubbs, Clennery Tubbs. Come and have a pint.'

Over the pint Tubbs talked about his invention. It was a cream that prevented the windows of cars from misting or frosting up, not just for a few hours or even for a day, but for several months. After that you put on some more cream. 'Firm tested it out. Worked perfectly. Even Jenner said so.'

'What was wrong then?'

'Inter Commerce make a windscreen wiping cloth, new pattern, big sales. Offered me five hundred to buy up my cream, then scrap it.'

'That's really dishonest.'

'Should have known better. Jenner's

jealous.'

'You can offer it to another firm.'

'He'd see I got the sack. Couldn't afford to take the chance. Like to see Wypitklere?'

'What's that?'

'Wipe it clear, see? Name it's patented under, mustn't use the actual spelling of words. I said, like to see it?'

The demonstration took place on a moist, misty day. They set out for a drive in Tubbs's small car, and before they left he wiped over the screen with Wypitklere. The screen remained clear throughout the drive when, as Tubbs triumphantly pointed out, the windscreens of almost all the cars they passed were misted over. Arthur was impressed but not yet convinced.

'Try it on your own car,' Tubbs said almost angrily.

Arthur was compelled to admit that he had no car. At one time Clare had driven a car but after being involved in an accident in which the other driver had been seriously injured she gave up motor cars for ever. She had made it clear to Arthur before their marriage that she would not expect her husband to drive or possess one, and at the time this had seemed unimportant. In the end Tubbs gave him two small pots of the cream and Arthur used one on the windscreen of Payne's car and gave the other to their doctor, a man named Hubble. On Payne's car it worked like a charm.

'I really think you're on to something this time, old man,' Payne had said, and he had implied that the bank might even consider giving it financial support.

Financial support was what Tubbs required. He was insistent that he must on no account be telephoned at Inter Commerce, and they always met in pubs. It was a different pub every time and Tubbs, who was a rather seedy little man, always looked nervously around. He said that somebody else was interested in the idea.

'They're talking about putting up five thousand quid for a twenty per cent interest. Could you meet that?'

'I'm afraid not.'

'Money's not important,' Tubbs said, rather to Arthur's surprise, for he had gathered the distinct impression that the other was in need of it. Tubbs ran a hand through his hair so that it stood up like a golliwog's, and stroked his rather indeterminate little beard. 'What I mean, Brownjohn, I'd consider less cash and a bigger percentage for myself.'

'If this stuff does all you say why don't you develop it on your own, borrow from your bank?' Arthur asked, with what he felt to be considerable shrewdness.

Tubbs moved his glass of beer about uneasily. Then, as if coming to a decision, he looked up and met Arthur's gaze. He had an intermittent pant like that of an exhausted dog, which he attributed to a weak heart, or in his own words a funny ticker. His eyeballs were enormous. 'Must be straight. I've got a record.'

'You've been in prison!'

'Right. Bank won't touch me, can't get backing, wouldn't be trying to sell Wypitklere if I could develop it myself. Strictly confidential, keep it to yourself, Jenner would have me out in a minute if he knew.'

'What was the offence?'

'I was *accused* of embezzlement. It was all a mistake.'

Somehow this admission convinced Arthur of Tubbs's good faith, perhaps because he felt that nobody would admit that he had been in prison if he were intending to commit a fraud afterwards. Money, however, was the problem. Payne had again spoken glowingly of the cream, but if money was to be borrowed from the bank Clare would have to know about it, and he knew that she would never agree. After much discussion Tubbs had said that he would take a thousand pounds for a twenty per cent share of all profits, but where was the money to come from? Easonby Mellon had to provide for two homes. There was very little money in his bank account, only just over five hundred pounds in the joint account Arthur shared with Clare. It was when he thought of the harmless deception that he practised in the role of Easonby Mellon that Arthur contemplated extending that deception. He flattered himself (or rather, he did not flatter himself) that he had some skill as a copyist, and Clare's signature was almost as familiar to him as his own. She had recently received the quarterly bank statement for the money in her private account, which he knew to be a considerable sum. He signed Clare's name to a cheque for five hundred pounds, which he transferred from her private to their joint account.

Looking back afterwards he thought that he must have been temporarily mad, but at the time he could think of nothing but getting a share of Wypitklere, and he persuaded himself that the deception would never be discovered. By the time she got her next quarterly statement at the end of June he would be able to repay the money through a loan. He would even repay it with a hundred pounds' interest, so that if she noticed the unauthorised withdrawal her anger would be changed to pleasure.

The agreement was signed in the office of a solicitor named Eversholt, who had drawn it up. He appeared to regard Arthur, and indeed the whole affair, with an air of faint astonishment, and pronounced the name Wypitklere as though it were a bad joke. In the end Tubbs agreed to increase Arthur's share of profits to twenty-five per cent. It seemed to him that he had driven a hard bargain, and he was pleased that Tubbs appeared satisfied.

'Here's my hand, partner.' Tubbs's hand was rather damp. 'What are the development plans?'

Arthur had not really considered this problem, beyond feeling that it must be possible to get backing for such an obvious winner in half a dozen places. Tubbs, however, did not seem disturbed by his vagueness. 'We'll be in touch then. Cheeribye,' he said. It did not occur to Arthur until afterwards that there was anything valedictory about his tone.

The blow fell within a week. Arthur had had several pots of Wypitklere made up from the formula given him by Tubbs, and had spent some time in making sketches for a wrapper to go round the container. He had also worked out on paper the costing of several thousand pots of the cream, the profitable retail price allowing for a handsome discount to distributors, and the likely profits. This delightful planning was disturbed by a telephone call from Payne. He asked Arthur, in a tone lacking his usual false joviality, to come and see him at home on the following morning.

When Arthur arrived Payne led him to the garage. He said nothing, but pointed to the windscreen and other glass sections of his car.

Arthur stared, aghast. In some places the glass was streaked as if somebody had drawn a cutting knife across it, and in others it was deeply pitted as though some glass-eating animal had been burrowing within it.

'Well?' the bank manager said.

Arthur wanted to say that it was not his fault, but what he actually said was, 'I can't explain it.'

Payne nodded grimly, as though this was what he had expected to hear. 'You don't deny that your *invention* is responsible for this.'

'I suppose it must be.'

'I shall have new glass put in throughout the car, and I shall charge it to you.'

'Of course. Of course, yes, please do.'

'Very well. I should have known better. In the meantime, I can't use my car.'

'I can't think what's gone wrong.' He had hardly known what he was saying, but the full horror of his situation was borne in upon him. 'I hope there isn't any reason—I hope you won't mention this to Clare.'

As Payne said to his wife afterwards, in that moment he felt really sorry for the poor little beggar, angry as he had been when he discovered the state of the glass. That his first thought should have been not of the failure of his invention, but the need to keep that failure from his wife. It was pathetic. 'Served me right, really,' he said to her philosophically. 'I should have known that anything he invented was bound to be a dud. You can't help liking Arthur, but he hasn't got much in the top storey.' They both made a point of being particularly nice to Arthur afterwards, and never mentioned a word about the matter to Clare.

Arthur went home a stricken man. He talked to the firm of wholesale chemists who had been making up Wypitklere and told them what he was using it for. They told him that the agent which cleared the windscreen had a corrosive effect upon glass. He paid a visit to Inter Commerce and saw the objectionable Jenner, but he was not really surprised to learn that no Clennery Tubbs had ever worked for them. He timidly recalled the occasion on which his dishwasher had been tested and Jenner remembered the man, who had come to show him some kind of demisting cream. Jenner had seen something similar before, and had not been taken in. Arthur saw the solicitor, who shrugged his shoulders and said that he had been approached simply to draw up an agreement and knew nothing about Tubbs. He went to the address given on the agreement and found that it was a tobacconist's, a mere accommodation address. The man remembered Tubbs but said that he had not been in for some time. He realised that Tubbs had spotted him for a possible gull when he came out from the demonstration and had taken advantage of Arthur's mistaken belief that he worked for Inter Commerce. He had been the victim of an obvious confidence trick.

The effect upon him was, superficially at

least, an odd one. He felt angry about Tubbs, but his bitterest feeling was reserved for Clare. At the back of his mind, as he now dimly realised, there had been a belief that one day he would be free of his thralldom to her, one day an invention would make a lot of money and the money would give him freedom. Now this would never happen. He had no faith any longer that he would ever make money out of an invention, and just a few weeks ahead of him there loomed the terrible day of reckoning when Clare received her quarterly statement.

CHAPTER FIVE

RIGHT APPROACH?

Arthur had often thought of abandoning the Lektreks office, but he had always decided against it. There was still a certain amount of business which came in automatically, and it helped to maintain his commercial identity. Supposing that one of his Fraycut acquaintances decided to pay him a visit, there was the office and there, during part of every day, was Arthur with the appurtenances of office life around him. He spent much of his time there in reading about old murder cases. He had always been fascinated by the idea of a murder so dazzlingly ingenious that its perpetrator could never be convicted even though his identity was known. He had a cupboard filled with volumes from the Notable British Trials series, and he read them again and again, observing where these aspirants to perfection had gone wrong. After the idea of Clare's death had come to him he jotted down some notes in the black-covered diary, which he brought up to London in his brief-case:

DIARY

Problem. *A wishes to dispose of C. He inherits money, will be obvious suspect.* But: *A's reputation is such that suspicion will not be automatic.* Conclusion: *A must proceed by a course avoiding usual means i.e. death must appear either natural or somehow completely detached from him.*

Why do I write like that, all rubbish? A and C. If a man can't be honest with himself in his diary there's nothing left for him. I want to see Clare dead. (Waited five minutes before I could write that down. Having written it I feel better, relieved. Know I shan't do it, only write. I've never done anything I wanted.)

Consider it, though. How would A. Brownjohn do this? Nothing easier. Obtain gelignite, fit it to vacuum cleaner, cleaner switched on, up goes she. But suppose Susan used the cleaner first?

Second idea. Clare often uses motor mower. Make ditto arrangement with it, simple enough. Mower and Clare vanish together. Yes?

Or electric shock, but not in bathroom, played out. Do it through electric iron in kitchen, fix wire so that she touches it while she's doing some washing? Think again, A. Brownjohn. Not advisable.

Why not? Too ingenious. A. Brownjohn is known to be a bit of an inventor, always fiddling with gadgets. If Clare's thoroughly shocked or blows up (joke) friends will say: 'Ah ha, Arthur B plays with racing cars, invented a dishwasher, etc. He's the man, needn't look further.' Somebody tells the police.

Stick to old favourites then and make a note, you must use nothing original, nothing mechanical.

Be honest with yourself, AB. You can write and you can think, but you're not going to do it.

Safety valve.

He finished the diary entry, which was less coherent than usual, and closed the book. But he went on thinking. He was precluded by natural dislike of shedding blood from anything that involved the use of an axe, hatchet or bludgeon. A gun might be clean and humane, but he neither possessed nor was skilled in using one. Drowning was ruled out by the fact that Clare had a firm objection to going in or upon the water.

The longer Arthur thought, the more he became convinced that he would be wise to stick to those old favourites, fire or poison. He considered, as he had often done before, the Rouse and Armstrong cases, and the Croydon murders.

He may have been drawn to Rouse and Armstrong by the similarity between their situations and his own. Rouse had tried to escape the burden of a bigamous marriage and not merely two but several establishments, as well as a number of maintenance orders, by setting fire to his car with a body in it that he hoped would be identified as his own. The body was thought to be that of a tramp whom he had met. Like Arthur, Rouse had wanted to start a new life, but what absurd mistakes he had made! Letting himself be seen climbing out of a ditch after setting fire to the car, and then going straight off to one of his girl friends. Arthur would never have been so foolish. The case fascinated him, but he had to acknowledge that even if he could have brought himself to kill a completely harmless stranger, the result would not really be what he wanted. It was true that he could simply disappear, but the truth was that he did not fancy being Easonby Mellon for ever. When you came right down to it, he had to admit that he wanted the money of which Clare had so unfairly deprived him by keeping it in her personal account, and if he wanted the money Arthur Brownjohn could not disappear.

He considered Armstrong, the timid little solicitor who had borne so meekly his wife's rebukes about his smoking and drinking, and had killed her by the use of arsenic. Here again he was struck at every re-reading by the stupid mistakes that had led to Armstrong's downfall. With his objective successfully achieved, what must he do but try to poison a rival solicitor! And the carelessness of leaving a packet of arsenic in one of his pockets was really inexcusable. If only he had been content with a death that had been certified as heart disease, if only he had not been subject to the hubris that seems so often to affect the successful poisoner. The Croydon poisonings showed what could be done by somebody whose feelings remained firmly under control. Here, in 1929, three members of a united family had died, one probably by arsenic put into his beer, another by arsenic in her soup, the third by arsenic in her tonic. Nobody had been tried, let alone convicted, for these crimes, and—this was the really vital point that must be latched on to—the first two deaths had been certified as due to natural causes and there would have been no trouble at all had not the mark been overstepped by a third death. Again, there was no question of Arthur's going on from one person to another in such an unreasonable, and as it might almost be called orgiastic manner. And there was one decisive point in favour of poison. In both the Armstrong and Croydon cases the doctors concerned had been friendly with the families, and had therefore been readier than they might otherwise have been to give a death certificate. At this point Arthur thought of old Doctor Hubble, and a warm delicious sense came to him that his problem was solved. He made a further diary note:

'The *modus operandi* is ordered by the means that are to hand.' He admired the phrase, which seemed to him like a maxim of Napoleon's. Doctor Hubble was the means and the *modus operandi* would therefore be poison, although it would probably be desirable to avoid arsenic. When Arthur had settled this he felt much easier in his mind. He donned the clothing of Major Easonby Mellon, and went to meet Miss Patricia Parker.

'Your secretary's out again,' she said when she arrived.

'Yes. The fact is you're rather a special case, Pat. I've got half a dozen names here, and I can give you them if you like, but frankly they're not good enough for you.' She did not comment on this, but smoothed her skirt over her knees. 'You said you weren't working?'

'Not at the moment.'

'I'm wondering if we can't find some

58

crackerjack job.'

'I can find a job easily enough. I thought this was a matrimonial agency, not an employment bureau.'

'So it is.' The Major laughed heartily. 'But you present a problem we don't often meet, Pat. I'll be frank and say I find you damned attractive personally. I was hoping you'd come to lunch with me again today.'

She looked at him and said, with complete self-possession, 'Are you married?'

It was an automatic reflex that made him say he was not. She nodded, and they went to lunch at the little place round the corner. This time she did not comment on the service, drank her share of the wine, and accepted the brandy that he offered to follow it. When he murmured over the brandy about somewhere he knew, she interrupted him. 'Your flat?'

Such brusqueness slightly disconcerted him. 'As a matter of fact it's a hotel. Very discreet, I can assure you.' She simply nodded again.

Over lunch he had been making a reassessment of her, and had come to the conclusion that she did not want to get married but simply wanted a man. Such a phenomenon was not unknown to him, and her conduct in the hotel room (it was the same hotel to which he had taken Joan and other ladies) confirmed this hypothesis. They stayed there until six o'clock, and he reflected at one point that the things she had refused to do for

Parker must have been very unusual. Perhaps there was no Parker, he thought sleepily, perhaps she had been telling lies, but what did it matter? He closed his eyes, and opened them again to find her unmistakably ready for another bit of nonsense.

'You're finished.'

'No no,' he said gallantly. Major Easonby Mellon was never finished. It could not be denied however that he was distinctly exhausted when they parted, and not wholly sorry when she said that she had to be out of London for three or four days and would get in touch with him when she returned. When he got back to Joan he ate the enormous meal she had cooked and then fell asleep in the arm-chair watching television. That night in bed she dug him in the ribs.

'I'll tell you one thing, E.'

'What's that?'

'All these books now, they keep saying there's no romance in being an agent, but I'll tell you what, there's no romance in being an agent's wife. It's just plain dull.'

He did not reply. He was thinking about being married to Pat, which might be exhausting but would also be exciting. Then he began to think about Doctor Hubble.

*　　　*　　　*

Doctor Hubble was a hairy man. Hair

60

sprouted from his ears, nostrils and wrists and, although he must have been sixty years old, a thick thatch of glossy black hair lay on his head. He was big, red-faced, and had the reputation of being still a very useful golfer and a hard drinker. Tales of his going round to see patients when he was so drunk that he was hardly able to walk straight or write a prescription were legion, and Arthur had had confirmation of this on one occasion when Clare had influenza and Hubble came round to see her reeking of whisky. It was generally believed that he had once diagnosed acute appendicitis as a bit of a stitch from too much exercise, and that the patient had died. Clare liked him because she had known him for years and he was, as she said, a proper doctor who came when you asked him and had a real bedside manner, not like these young whippersnappers who just looked at you and then prescribed some drug or other. Doctor Hubble was a great man for a good old-fashioned bottle of tonic. His capacity for the part Arthur meant him to play was confirmed as soon as they began to talk in Hubble's sitting-room.

'You'll have a drop of the hard stuff.' He barely waited for assent before pouring two liberal tots of whisky. 'And if you take my advice you won't spoil it with soda.' Arthur, who did not much like whisky and preferred soda to plain water, meekly took what he was given. 'You said this wasn't a professional visit.'

'I owe you an apology.' Hubble stared at him. 'About Wypitklere.'

'Wipe it clear? Oh, you mean that stuff for the car. Your invention.' He laughed as if this were a joke. 'Tell you the truth I haven't used it yet. Slipped my mind.'

'That's good. I've discovered a small flaw in the formula, it doesn't work quite as it should on certain types of glass. I don't think you should use it. Perhaps you'd let me have it back.'

The doctor rooted about uncertainly in a desk that was filled to overflowing with papers. Then he shouted for his wife, a thin wispy woman whose pallor provided a strong contrast to his abundant vitality. 'Know where that whatyemaycallit is, tin of stuff Brownjohn here gave me a few days ago? Hope I haven't given it to someone for rheumatism.' He roared with laughter.

The tin proved to be in the garage. When it was back in Arthur's possession Hubble suggested another drink.

'Thank you. Not quite so strong this time.' He saw with pleasure that the doctor gave himself another generous measure. 'There's something else I wanted to mention. I'm a little worried about Clare.' He launched into an exaggerated description of the gastric symptoms from which Clare said she suffered.

'I wondered if you could come round and give her a check-up without, you know, mentioning that I'd been in to see you.'

'Of course, of course. Let's see, to-day's Friday. I'm playing a round on Sunday morning. What say I look in afterwards, we met in the street and you asked me in for a drink before lunch? Don't suppose there's anything in it, but no harm in taking a looksee.' Arthur assented. A visit after Hubble had played a round of golf and had several drinks in the club-house should be ideal.

A hasty study of medical manuals had left him undecided about what poison it would be advisable to use, but he carried out these preliminary moves with what seemed to him considerable ingenuity. Clare used a tooth powder, not paste. Arthur had bought a jar of this and spent some of the time in replacing about half of the contents with powdered *nux vomica*. The change in appearance was almost undetectable, and on Friday night he substituted his jar for the one in the bathroom cabinet. The results were gratifying. Clare was slightly sick in the middle of the night and sick again in mid-morning. The beauty of this device was that he could end the sickness whenever he wished by replacing the harmless tooth powder. He did this on Saturday night, and then put back the powder containing *nux vomica* again on Sunday morning. Clare was sick during the morning, and when Hubble

63

arrived she was ready to be examined and to tell him her symptoms in detail.

The doctor was upstairs with her for thirty minutes. When he came down he said, 'I'll take that drop of the hard stuff you were offering.' His eyes were slightly bloodshot. He drank half the whisky at a gulp. 'That's better.'

'What do you think?'

'Wrong eating.'

'What's that?'

Hubble glared at him. 'I said, wrong eating. All these filthy health foods. I've told her so.'

'But I thought they were good for you.'

'They may be good for *some people*.' Hubble sounded as though he were referring to Trobriand islanders. 'Not for her. She needs red meat. What did she have last night? Grated stuff.'

'I had it too.'

The doctor ignored that. 'I've put her on a high protein diet.'

'But there's nothing serious?'

'Nothing at all.'

Clare was more indignant than upset, but small steaks and chops made their appearance on the table and her attacks of sickness ceased. A brilliant idea had come to Arthur about the *modus operandi*—he did not care, even in his mind, to use the word poison. It had been given him by Hubble and it was especially gratifying because it fulfilled the maxim that out of defeat shall come forth victory. The ingredient in Wypitklere that had produced such drastic effects on glass was zincalium, a derivative of a metallic acid based on zinc. Would it not be possible to use zincalium as the *modus operandi*? On Tuesday morning Arthur left to take up his mid-week residence at Clapham. He left Clare the tooth powder containing *nux vomica* so that she might be satisfyingly sick in his absence. Perhaps she would call in Hubble, perhaps not. It really didn't matter. When he returned next week-end he hoped to resolve the Clare situation for good.

CHAPTER SIX

WRONG EFFECT

Nobody loves a poisoner. In the long lists of means of murder it would probably be true to say that poison is the method most generally abhorred and despised. People will express sympathy with axe-killers, stranglers, gunmen, even with those who chop their victims' bodies into bits, but not with poisoners. Yet Armstrong was thought of by acquaintances as an agreeable little man, and Crippen was in many respects amiable. Some poisoners like Neill Cream are far from agreeable characters, but many more are commonplace, emotionally undeveloped people who find themselves in a position from which murder by poison seems the only, or at least the simplest, way out. Once this has been decided the controls operating in their everyday life cease to be effective. So Arthur stopped thinking about Clare as a person at all, and managed to regard her as solely an object to be removed.

He spent a large part of his three days at Clapham reading about the effects of zincalium and deciding on the best way of using it. 'If zincalium is used with sufficient care and cunning for homicidal purposes we may get a succession of mild attacks of the acute symptoms with remissions,' he read in one text-book. There was no time for that, but happily the tooth powder should serve the same purpose of providing a case history which stretched back a little way in time. If there was one aspect of the affair that gave him satisfaction it was the ingenuity of using a preliminary emetic that was perfectly harmless. Had that been done before? He thought not. He was pleased to learn that zincalium was not an exceptionally painful poison. It was accompanied by 'nausea, vomiting, general uneasiness and depression,' but did not cause a burning sensation or have the drastic effects of some other metallic poisons. It would have been pleasant to use a drug that caused Clare to cease upon the midnight with no pain, thereby avoiding all unpleasantness, but one must use the means that are to hand. What really disturbed him was the possibility that he might not be able to distil enough zincalium out of the Wypitklere to achieve the desired result. He distilled the zincalium in the kitchen at Elm Drive while Joan looked on, fascinated.

'E, whatever are you doing?'

'Distilling this, my dear.'

'I see that, but what's it for?'

He looked up. 'You've heard me talk about Flexner in the department?'

'The expert in all those terrible germs and poisons. But I thought he was down at that place, what is it, Porton?'

'Most of the time he is, but he's been in the office recently, advising the Chief about disposing of a rather awkward customer, a Rumanian. He's given some advice which the Chief is slightly doubtful about, and I'm just checking one of his conclusions. You know what the Chief's like. He thinks someone from the other side may have got at Flexner.'

He poured the mixture into a beaker. 'If everything's in order there should be a sediment at the bottom and a colourless liquid at the top.' He watched the sediment settle with satisfaction, strained off the liquid above it, and poured it away.

'Is that the way it should be? That powder?'

'Precisely.'

'So Flexner hasn't been got at?'

'Evidently not.'

'The Chief knows he can rely on you, doesn't he?'

He shook his head. 'Not a bit of it. He's probably got somebody else checking my conclusions. It may even be that this bit of research is a blind, and that we're going to use quite a different method to deal with our Rumanian friend. But if the Chief hasn't been fooling me there is enough of this powder here to kill a hundred people.'

Here he was being optimistic, for the truth was that the text-books he had consulted were extremely vague about the amount of zincalium needed. He would have to experiment, that was all. After the powder had dried he divided it carefully, putting the larger quantity into one envelope and the smaller into another. He sealed both packets and put the two of them into one big Manila envelope. Shades of Armstrong! But there was this difference, that he would burn the envelope immediately after use. No tell-tale traces would be found in *his* pockets.

'A hundred people. Oh, E, I wish you could get out of it.' Joan was almost in tears. He stroked her hair.

'Sometimes I wish I could too. But once you're in the service, you're in it for life.'

DIARY
Sunday May 18

2 a.m. Sitting at my desk. Peaceful. Just been down to see Clare. She is sleeping quietly, one hand clutching the coverlet. Stood looking at her, all colour gone from her face leaving it like milk. She seemed very young, I felt sorry for her. But the person I have to feel sorry for is myself. I have ruined everything.

After Hubble had gone this evening I thought about my life and saw it as a record of failure. I have never done anything that succeeded, never carried through any idea, although I do believe I have had some good ones. Sometimes I have been really stupid, as I was about the cleaning cream. I trust people too much. I remember Mother putting her hand on my head and saying she hoped I should find somebody to look after me, because that was what I should need in life. I didn't understand her then, but do now. Remember also Roberts, headmaster at the grammar school, telling Mother that I lacked resolution. He was right. Sometimes it seems to me that what we do is a matter of the way we look. If I looked different I should be different. I think I have proved that through EM.

Putting it down here may make me feel better. Tonight shan't be able to sleep. Desperate.

Came back on Friday, asked Clare how she had been. Tuesday night she had been sick, she said, Wednesday morning sick again. Said perhaps she'd had too much protein after all, had she rung Hubble?

'*I nearly rang him. And then I thought I should be able to find out what it was myself. Couldn't be the food. I'd been ill before that. And I did find out what it was.*'

'*What?*'

'*My tooth powder.*' *I was aghast, terrified. I stammered something, said it couldn't be. She gave me a glare of hideous triumph.*

'*Don't you see? Every time I brushed my teeth I was sick. There was something wrong with that tin, it must have been bad. I've changed to a tube, had no trouble since.*' *I asked what she had done with the tin and she said she'd thrown it away. Also said she would tell Hubble when she saw him to-morrow.*

'*To-morrow?*' *I must have looked foolish, but then she always thinks I look foolish. She said she had asked some people in for drinks, Hubble one of them.*

After thinking about this I realised that perhaps it was all to the good. When Hubble came I should be able to drop in a worried reference to her gastric trouble, even mention in a joking way her attribution of it to tooth powder. Then to-morrow night a small dose of Z in her nightcap. The large dose the following week-end.

We played bezique (let her win) and I made the nightcap and took it up. She said I made a good whisky toddy. Expect I looked strange at

70

that, because she went on: 'Not been drinking, have you?' I said of course not. 'It's for your own good I'm saying it, you know you can't drink.'

She put her hand on mine, then belched. I was disgusted, it was all I could do not to turn away my head. Her hand is very coarse with the veins standing out, actually it is bigger than my own hand which is small and rather delicate. There is something coarse altogether about her which I find repulsive.

That was Friday. Saturday was routine. Up at seven-thirty, breakfast, potter round the garden in old clothes, out with the shopping basket. Clare doesn't like me to go shopping. However. I like it so why shouldn't I do it? Why should I feel guilty as though I were letting her down, shopping isn't a thing a Slattery man would do?

Damn all Slatteries.

Remember thinking, soon I shall be able to go shopping without worrying, all on my owneo, buy what I like. That would be a real pleasure. I wonder if it's true that all the most intense pleasures are solitary? After all, I haven't joined a slot racing club. I say it's because Clare wouldn't like the members to come here, but perhaps it's because I like slot racing on my own.

Perhaps. Doesn't matter. The question's not going to arise.

3 o'clock. Wide awake.

Went to the supermarket in the High Street, marvellous place, met Mrs. Payne and of course she asked about Clare. Said she was better, saw my opportunity.

'I'm not quite satisfied, though. Do you know what she says caused the trouble? Her tooth powder.' Mrs. P stared, as well she might. 'She's thrown it out. I don't think tooth powder could cause sickness, do you?'

'I never heard of such a thing. Is she getting fancies?' To Mrs. P 'fancies' are like scarlet fever. Had a little talk with her about prices, very interesting. Corned beef in the supermarket is ninepence a tin cheaper than at Penquick's. I believe the day of the private grocer has gone. Went home feeling pleased with self at mentioning powder. A good general is a bold general I thought.

Drinks in the evening, representative Fraycut selection. Payne and wife, retired naval commander named Burke, Charles Ransom secretary of local Liberal Party, one or two others. And of course Hubble plus wife, H smelling of drink. Susan handed round hot sausages and bits of things on toast, I looked after drinks. Had one or two. Told tooth powder story to people, including Hubble, asked him what he thought, had the powder caused the trouble?

He glared at me, made me feel uncomfortable. 'Told you what I thought.' He said something about high protein diet.

I was going to ask him how he explained the tooth powder and have another drink when Clare put her hand over mine (again!) and said I'd had enough. Caught sight of self in a glass, tie askew and head shining, was inclined to agree. I knew I had to keep absolutely clear-headed, in command of events. Clare introduced me to a ghastly man named Elsom, engineering executive, face full of teeth, recently come to Fraycut, Clare met him at some Liberal do. Conversation:

E   How's it going, old man?
Self Very well, thanks.
E   Must have a bit of lunch one day. I mean, we're more or less in the same line, I believe. What's your office number?
Self I'm in quite a small way, you know.
E   Still, I'd like to have a natter. Might be useful. Nothing too small to interest GBD.
Self GBD?
E   Gracey, Basinghall and Derwent. My outfit. They tell me you're by way of being an inventor.
Self Just an amateur.
E   Don't be modest. You must make your money out of something.

Obviously a pest. But I've dealt with people like this before, have a good technique of brushing them off, even though I say so. Introduced him now to Mrs. Payne who started on at once about disgraceful English weather and their holiday in Spain. Had to give Elsom office number but got away after that. Subsequent technique will be to say I have another engagement if he rings, and if I'm not there then naturally there's no reply.

Half an hour later they'd all gone. Clare in a filthy temper when we cleared things away, seemed to think I'd had too much.

'Arthur, how many times have I told you not to take more than two glasses?' Couldn't say my dear. Unanswerable question. Didn't try to answer it. 'A glass filled with tonic water looks just the same as one filled with gin. No Slattery has been unable to hold his liquor, but you are not a Slattery.' Unanswerable again. 'I remember when Uncle Ratty was out in Africa . . .'

Soon I shall be free of this, I told myself, I shall never hear the name Slattery again. Parties like these tire Clare out, and at ten-thirty she said she was going to bed. Self: 'I'll bring up your nightcap.' Somehow I felt it was certain she would say she was too tired this evening, but she simply nodded.

Got the small Manila envelope out of brief-case. Made the drink. Hand trembling? Not at all. Put powder carefully into it, dissolved almost at once. Didn't cloud the glass which stood, browny-gold, steaming a little. Took it up. I still believed something would happen to stop her drinking it, but nothing did. Afterwards all she said was: 'Rather strong.'

'I mixed it as usual.'

Brought down glass, washed it, put envelope back in brief-case (too soon to burn, think of smell), and relocked. Came up here, sat down to write diary, couldn't because of excitement. Analysed my own feelings. To do something that causes pain to another person, I've always believed that to be wrong. I am not a cruel man. That is the truth. But think of the way Clare has behaved to me, that's what is responsible for my actions. The truth is I really cannot think of her as a person at all. She is an object, an obstacle. I have done my best to treat her well, but it is impossible. Summing up my analysis, I have to say that what I felt was a sense of achievement.

I was wrong.

(Just been down to look at her again. The thought crossed my mind that she might be dead. Thought, believed, hoped, what is the word? Nonsense, I knew it wouldn't be so. She was sleeping quietly.)

Settled down to wait. Went to see her, she was asleep. Came down, took all the sitting-room ornaments into the kitchen and washed them, something to do. Had just decided nothing would happen when there was a noise upstairs. Then moaning. Went up. She was on the landing outside the bathroom bent almost double, retching. Got her out into the lavatory—but I can't write about all that, it disgusts me. She was in pain, and that is something I can't bear. Rang Hubble. It seemed a terribly long time before he arrived, just before midnight. She went on being sick. He was drunk, I'm sure of it. Had to hold on to the rail as he came upstairs. Left him with Clare. Twenty minutes before he came down. Knew what he'd say, severe gastric upset. Offered a drink, but he refused!! Had one myself. Then the conversation. Said, how is she?

H   *Washed out her stomach, given her an injection, she's asleep. (Then terrible glare) What did she have to-night?*

Self *You were at the party, you saw for yourself. (Nice touch.) I'm afraid she sometimes drinks more than is good for her, with her stomach.*

H   *Afterwards?*

Self *Nothing afterwards. Except her usual nightcap, hot whisky and lime juice. (Boldly) I made it for her.*

H   *Glass.*

Self *What's that?*

H   *Glass, man, where's the glass?*

Self *I washed it up and put it away.*

H   *Ha (Two letters only, but an awful sound.) Bottles.*

I got him the bottles of whisky and lime juice. He sniffed, tasted, recorked them. I thought of saying 'You should know the smell of whisky if anyone does,' but didn't of course. Had to say something though, asked if it was

76

gastric attack. I shall never forget his reply.

'If you call poisoning gastric.'

Poisoning! What a dreadful word! Don't know how I managed to look at him, but I did. I even managed to say something about it being possibly one of the canapés. He answered as if he were talking to a child, didn't sound at all drunk.

'When I saw your wife recently there was nothing at all seriously wrong with her.' I said quietly that she had been sick. 'I said nothing serious. Now she's had a violent stomach upset, caused by something she's eaten or drunk. The two things aren't connected. I've an impression it was something corrosive, a mild solution of some metallic poison possibly. Something she drank would be more likely than food.'

'I don't see what it could be.'

'Mystery then. But she'll do, no need to worry. I'll look in to-morrow. Be careful what she eats and drinks for the next day or two. I'll tell her when I see her. But you might bear it in mind too.'

Harmless words? But they weren't, I know they weren't. I know they were a warning. He is not the fool he looks, he knew. But why should this happen to me? In the Croydon case the doctors never had any doubt it was gastric trouble, any more than Armstrong's doctor had any doubt. Why should I be so unlucky? I'm sure that anyone would have

77

thought as I did about Hubble.

When he had left I knew I dare not go on. Unlocked brief-case, took out rest of Z, flushed it down the lavatory, burned both envelopes. All right then. But what happens now? I must write out the words of my humiliation plainly.

I have failed.

CHAPTER SEVEN

THE MAN FROM UGLI

Clare made a quick recovery. He seemed to spend Sunday in making little milky dishes and taking them up to her. Hubble paid a visit on Sunday afternoon and expressed himself satisfied with her progress but still mystified by the origin of her illness. His manner was neither friendly nor hostile. The only solace was the slot racing layout. Arthur spent most of the afternoon in the attic, rearranging the track to make a Silverstone circuit and putting the pits and spectator stands into new positions. He did not race the cars because Clare was having a nap, and he was afraid of waking her.

By Monday morning she was up and about the house. She attributed her illness to Hubble's unwisdom in urging her to eat bloody bits of meat and other heavy foods, and her return to semi-vegetarianism began on Monday evening with a dish of grated cheese and carrots. On Tuesday morning Arthur gratefully escaped, telling her that he had an important engagement in Bristol, followed by a tour of the West country. He had more or less recovered what he thought of as his poise. Something, he said to himself in the train on the way up from Fraycut to Waterloo, something will have to be done. But what? In a sense there was no need to do anything at all, for it was hardly likely that, when Clare received her bank statement, she would take legal action against him. He rehearsed in the train a dialogue in which he rebutted her complaints of fraud and forgery. 'You have only yourself to blame ... a wife's money should belong to her husband ... if you had not deliberately denied me the capital I needed to develop my inventions ...'

He shook his head sadly. All that might be true, but it really did not matter if it was, because he would never be able to bring himself to say such things. He saw instead a future in which Clare's domination over him would be unbearably complete.

On this Tuesday he found it difficult to slip into the personality of Easonby Mellon. He did not open the post with his usual zest nor interview clients with his customary conviction. The shadow of Arthur Brownjohn hung over him like a heavy cold, and it was only partly dispelled after a telephone call made to Clare to say that he had found it impossible to postpone his West country tour—he had promised that he would try to do so—and would not be home until Friday. He had four days of freedom, but what were they worth? It was a gloomy Easonby Mellon who went home that evening to Clapham and to Joan. A bit of nonsense revived him slightly, and the meal of liver and bacon followed by steamed sultana pudding which they ate afterwards confirmed him in a feeling that life might have its silver lining. They sat out in the little back garden listening to the purring lawn mower next door. The sound induced a sense of peace. He closed his eyes and did not hear her properly when Joan said something. He asked her to repeat it.

'I said, having ructions at the office?'

There was something odd about her tone. He opened his eyes. Her face wore what she no doubt thought of as a cryptic smile. He said with an effort, 'If I've been out of sorts it's not because—'

'I wondered. Because he's been here.'

'Who?'

She looked round, leaned over and whispered. 'The man from UGLI.'

Was she out of her mind? Was there to be no peace even in Clapham? He sat up in the deck-chair. 'Joan, what are you talking about?'

'It was exciting. Tell me, what does he look like?'

'What does *who* look like?'

'Flexner. I'm sure that's who it was.'

He restrained an impulse to say that she was talking nonsense. How had he described Flexner? 'He's tall, over six foot, always dressed like a city man, dark grey or blue suit, umbrella and bowler hat—'

She was nodding. 'He hadn't got the bowler hat, but that's right. And you said he was swarthy.'

'Dark. Not swarthy.'

'And a pigeon-toed walk, you mentioned that. Very sinister, I thought he was.'

He was suddenly angry at this tomfoolery. 'It can't have been Flexner.'

'Oh, I'm sure it was. Why not?'

'He's out of the country. What did this man say?'

'But E, I feel sure—'

'What did he *say*?' He was almost shouting. She looked alarmed. 'Let's go inside.'

In the flat she described him. 'He was a tall man, swarthy, and he asked for you so I said you weren't here, and then he said he wanted to contact you urgently and I thought I recognised him from your description so I said, "You're attached to the Department, aren't you?" I thought, you see, it wouldn't mean anything to him if he weren't. And he smiled, and it was one of those smiles you said he could give, that cut like a razor, and he said, "You might say I'm attached, yes." So then I told him I expected he'd know where to find you and *he* said, "Ah yes, but there's been a spot of trouble, I didn't want to contact him there." So I said I couldn't help him and then I knew who he was and I said, "You're Mr. Flexner, aren't you?" and he said with another smile, "That's right." So then I said would he leave a message, but he just said tell you that he would be in touch when the time came. I'm sorry if I did wrong, E.'

'You didn't do wrong.' He let the waves of her talk move over him. In bed he felt such a chill of apprehension that he had to go out to the lavatory. On his return he did not go to sleep for a long time, and when he slept at last it was with one hand coiled tightly round the thumb of the other, a habit which belonged to his childhood.

At breakfast Joan talked about Flexner and the Department until he could bear it no longer, and shouted at her. She began to cry.

'You don't want me to have anything to do with your life. I'm just something to cook meals and go to bed with.' This was so nearly true that he found it difficult to answer. 'It's not like being your wife at all. I thought I was really going to be part of your life, but you won't let me. I hate the Department.'

'You're sure he didn't say anything else? About getting in touch, I mean.'

'No. Just when the time came. And he smiled. He's got a nasty smile, hasn't he?'

He agreed absently. 'Chin up, old girl. Sorry I can't tell you anything. It's the old struggle for power.'

'With AX, you mean?'

'AX is playing a part, but it's our own lot I'm worried about. There are moves to take us over, merge us with another department. That may be why Flexner was here.'

'You said he was out of the country.'

He said snappishly, 'Obviously I was wrong. Since he's come back it must be about something important.'

He left her eager for a further instalment of Department news. His room in Romany House held the usual bunch of letters and postal orders. He dealt with them efficiently, but that sense of impending doom lay heavy as a ball in his stomach. The morning was alleviated only by a telephone call from Pat. She asked if they could meet and when he invited her to lunch she said that she would be too late for that, but could meet him at three o'clock in the hotel. This bold declaration of the fact that her interest was purely sexual flattered him, and gave savour to the quick lunch he ate in a pub. It was an expectant Major Easonby Mellon who entered the hotel, to be told with a smirk that his wife was already there.

He found her on the edge of the bed in bra

and knickers, a cigarette in her mouth. She put out the cigarette at once but somehow her appearance on the bed, smoking and nearly naked, upset him. She looked, if he had to put the thing crudely, like a tart, and he wondered again why she had come to him. Sex, however, is a solvent for doubt, and by the time she had pulled him on to the bed and helped him to take off his clothes he was in no state to be concerned about her motives. He was astonished when she rolled off the bed and put on her knickers, which he had removed in the course of the scuffle. He was about to remonstrate when she jerked a thumb behind him. He turned.

A man was in the room with them. He was tall, thin and dark, he wore a dark grey suit, and he was smiling disagreeably. There could be little doubt that he was the man Joan had described as Flexner. In his hand there was a tiny camera, which he put away in his pocket. He nodded to Pat, who put on her frock. Then he said amiably enough, 'Hi. Time for you and me to have a talk. I'm Jack Parker, Pat's husband.'

Major Mellon felt at an enormous disadvantage without his clothes. He dressed quickly but in a fumbling manner, having difficulty with his trousers. His mind was empty of thought, he did not know what to say. Parker was quite at his ease.

'Little club round the corner. I'm a member.

No hurry. Talk round there when you're ready.'

Suppose I'm not prepared to come, suppose I say no to your little club, he thought. But he knew that he was not capable of this, that coming on top of everything else this misfortune had stunned him. He followed them obediently into a sordid basement club down a side street. The room was small and dirty, the barman was a Greek or Cypriot in need of a shave. Parker ordered three whiskies and they sat at a small table. He was completely self-possessed. He might have been talking about the weather.

'I'll put the position to you, Major, so that you know just where you are. First of all, the Major. You're not entitled to call yourself that, there's no Major Easonby Mellon in the Army List. Next your firm. You've got no licence to operate as you should have—I've checked— and you haven't got a secretary. You're only in the office part time. It's just a trick for making money. You've kidded your wife that you work for some mysterious Department or other, so I played along when I came last night.'

'Outrageous.' Major Mellon had found his voice, although it came through as a croak.

'I thought you'd be pleased.'

'How did you know where I lived?'

'Followed you. Been keeping an eye on you ever since the day Pat came along. Careless of you not to notice. Another point, I just

85

mention it in passing. You don't go home to Clapham every night. I'm only making a guess, but do you know what it smells like to me? It smells as though you've got a little love nest tucked away somewhere else.'

'He couldn't have,' the girl said. 'He hasn't got the guts.'

'Shut up. Am I right?'

Alarm struggled with relief, alarm that the man had got so near to the truth, relief that he had not discovered it. 'Of course not.'

Parker shrugged. 'I could easily find out, but to me it doesn't matter. This is a business deal.'

'The badger game.' He knew the phrase from books.

'Not really.' Parker smiled again. He looked like a large well-dressed rat. 'I sent Pat along thinking you might put her in touch with a rich mark. She's a clever girl. She spotted right away that you were a mark yourself.'

He sipped the whisky. It tasted disagreeably of oil. 'How do you mean?'

'Suppose it got through to the Greater London Council—they issue your licence, I've done my homework—that you're operating under a false title and without a licence. Suppose Pat makes a complaint about you and I back it up with these pictures you'd be for the high jump, agreed?'

'You'd never dare to do it.'

'We're clean. We've never been inside. The

point is, you wouldn't want us to do it. I'd lay odds Mellon's not your real name. I dare say the bogeys would be pleased to know where you are.'

With a sense of shock he realised that they thought he was a crook like themselves, operating a racket. The fact that this was in a sense true did not make him less indignant.

Parker went to the bar and brought back three more whiskies. The girl was becoming impatient. 'Get to it, Jack. You're too fond of the sound of your own voice.'

'We'll do it my way if you don't mind.' She flinched slightly. 'I want the Major here to know just where he stands. Then we can fix the deal.'

'The deal?'

'It's a business deal. I said so from the start, no hard feelings.'

He sipped the second whisky. The inside of his mouth seemed to be numb. 'What sort of deal?'

'Twenty a week.'

'Pounds?' He could not take it in. 'You want me to pay you twenty pounds each week?'

'Every Friday. One of us will drop in to collect. Probably me. You might forget yourself with Pat.' He smiled again.

'Impossible.'

'Don't say that. Let's keep it friendly.' Parker's mouth when he did not smile was like two lines of steel. 'I tell you what. There are

87

two ways of doing this. Twenty a week straight, and that's what I'd like. Or a fiver a week and you give Pat some introductions to marks.'

'No, I can't do that. I don't work in that way, I couldn't possibly—' He left the sentence unfinished.

'It would have advantages.' Parker was watching him. 'You'd get a cut. Twenty per cent. And you don't have to know anything about it, there'd be no trouble. Pat's clever. She can tell which ones to take. And you can trust me, I know how hard to squeeze.'

The walls of the room were lime green, and one was discoloured where damp had seeped through. They made him feel sick. 'That sort of thing, I can't involve myself in it.'

Parker took out a long thin cheroot from a case and lighted it. The cheroot stuck out sharply from a face composed of a series of angles. 'I'm being patient, Dad, but you haven't grasped it. You're over a barrel. You don't have a choice. It's twenty a week, or five and a little co-operation, a partnership. I'll be frank, we don't want trouble, but that's nothing to the way you don't want it.'

'I must have time to think.'

'No. Here and now.'

He seemed to be incapable of thought. Major Mellon had shrivelled to Arthur Brownjohn, and it was Arthur who said miserably, 'Five. And the—the co-operation.'

'Sensible.' Parker gripped his hand. 'Let's

get along.'

'Where to?'

'Where do you think? The office.'

The next hour was one of the most miserable in his life. They took a taxi to Romany House and went to the office of Matrimonial Assistance. He gave Parker five pound notes and then the Parkers went through his files, looking for possible marks and making rude comments. They picked out a dozen possibles, mostly elderly men who said that they had a private income, or middle-aged business men. He agreed to send them Pat's name, with a special recommendation.

'After that you have nothing to do with it. Leave it to Pat. She can size 'em up in ten minutes. The ones we want are married, out for a bit of fun on the side. They have their fun, but they pay for it. What's fairer than that?' Parker was in high good humour.

When they had gone he sat in the little office with his head on the table. The humiliation of watching them go through his files and read the letters on his desk was somehow the worst thing of all. The business he had built was dishonest, yet he took a pride in it and felt it to be something he had created. That he should have been forced to allow these crooks to use what he had done as a basis for their filthy game was hard to bear. He realised that this was what Parker had intended from the start, and that if he had agreed to pay twenty pounds a week something more would have been demanded of him. It was his list of gulls they were after, to make some quick killings. The future was foreseeable. The Parkers might bring off half a dozen coups, but at some time they would choose the wrong person and one of their marks would go to the police. They might be arrested or they might get away, but either way he would be dragged into it, and his complicity would be obvious. And of course his double life would be revealed by any serious police investigation. What sentence was likely for bigamy? In the general wreck of his fortunes that did not seem particularly important. Whichever way he looked, disaster lay ahead.

CHAPTER EIGHT

THE SOLUTION

The solution was simple enough in its essential elements, and it occurred to him almost immediately. It was that he must say good-bye to Major Easonby Mellon. What was he, after all, but a wig, a beard, some loud suits and an accompanying loud manner? If he were to disappear to-morrow who would be the wiser? The clients of Matrimonial Assistance would write letters, come to the office, and eventually no doubt report his absence to the company that ran Romany House. The company would write to him and get in touch with his bank, but he would have drawn out all except a nominal fragment of the money he had in credit. Joan might be approached, but what could she say except some tales about UGLI 3 and—a nice confirmatory touch—about the man who had come to see him? And who would suffer? Honesty compelled him to admit that Joan would be left high and dry. He felt sorry for her, but was able to console himself with the thought that she was the kind of woman who would always, somehow and somewhere, find a man. To live with men and be deceived by them was her destiny. No, the real sufferer would be—himself. If he was to go on living with Clare the emotional release afforded by Easonby Mellon was a necessity. And the suffering would not only be emotional. If Matrimonial Assistance closed down, what would Clare say when he told her that he could no longer pay the expenses of the household? He shivered at the thought of her endless wrath. The solution so simple in its essential elements was thus no solution at all.

On Thursday morning he sat brooding in the Lektreks office over a volume dealing with the James Camb case. Camb, a steward with the Union Castle had been accused of strangling a girl in her cabin and then pushing her body out of the porthole. He had no doubt relied upon the absence of a body, but he was found guilty just the same. If only, Arthur reflected, he could make Clare magically disappear so that her money came to him! But of course it was not possible. He closed the book with a sigh at the very moment that a knock sounded on the door. He opened it expecting to see the caretaker and was disconcerted to be confronted by the fine white teeth of—it took him a moment even to remember the man's name—Elsom, the engineering executive.

'Hallo there.' Almost imperceptibly Elsom was in the room, which he stared at quite frankly, his gaze passing like a rake over the dusty box files, the single desk with its typewriter, the gas ring for making tea, the blueprints of the Everlasting Torch and its successor the Hammerless Screw Inserter, the notices on the walls certifying that Lektreks was incorporated as a company and that Arthur was a member of the Society of Inventors. Elsom, carefully regarded, was an objectionable-looking man. He had close-cut sandy hair and a sandy moustache, vertical nostrils which seemed distended by curiosity, almost lashless eyes and extremely large square competent-looking hands. He was the sort of man who in that quick glance round would have photographed and permanently recorded anything possibly useful to him. 'So this is where you tuck yourself away,' Elsom said. 'I was passing by and thought I'd look in to see if you were free for a spot of lunch.'

Arthur intended to say that he was not, but reconsidered. He felt certain that something lay behind Elsom's casual dropping-in. If he was put off he might drop in again or become a pest on the telephone. There had been occasions, although they could be counted on the fingers of both hands, when people from Fraycut had visited the office, and Arthur had always firmly stressed that it was no more than a receiving place for correspondence, and had got them out of it as quickly as possible. Clare herself had been to the office only twice, conveying both her contempt for it and her astonishment that he was able to make a living from such a place. She had conceded that it was a good address, but the whole ambience was obviously a wretched one when put beside the Slattery connection. Arthur felt that it would be a good idea to get this grinning bristly Elsom out of the office and also to damp any curiosity he might be feeling. He said that a spot of lunch would be very nice.

They ate in a pub not far away. Elsom was known in the Grill Room. He took charge of the meal, giving particular instructions about the way in which their steaks should be done, and going into details about the wine. It struck Arthur that he was being treated with some attention. When the steaks came Elsom attacked his savagely, and kept up a flow of conversation about people in Fraycut until he had eaten the last scrap. Then he asked how things were going.

'Going? Oh, business you mean. I mustn't grumble.' He added untruthfully, 'Very glad you found me.'

'You don't put up much of a front.'

'What would be the point?' Arthur had countered this remark before. 'My business isn't done in London, it's personal.'

Most people left it at that but Elsom, at the same time that he gestured to a waiter to bring a tray with the puddings on it, said out of the side of his mouth, 'No girl to take messages.'

'It's difficult to get efficient staff. I use an answering service.'

Elsom nodded and transferred his interest to the trolley, ordering what proved to be a huge portion of trifle. He disposed of it in a few gulps and Arthur, toying uneasily with crême caramel, had the feeling that his companion needed something crunchy on which to sharpen his teeth. No wonder that a trifle was quickly disposed of. Elsom's next remark took him by surprise.

'Can't help feeling a bit sorry for old Clare.'

'You mean her illness? She was much better when I left yesterday.'

'Don't mean that. Being the grass widow was what I had in mind. I mean, you're away three, four nights a week.'

'Oh, not always. It varies.'

94

'If I were you I'd be feeling worried.' The words were alarming. What did the man mean? 'She's damned attractive, your good lady.'

'Clare?'

'I wouldn't go off and leave her half the week, I know that.' Elsom took a mouthful of scalding coffee and roared with laughter. 'Just pulling your leg, old man. Perhaps it's the other way round, eh? A few home comforts up in the Midlands?' He laughed again.

Those were the vital words, although their possible implications were not borne in upon him at the time. It had never crossed his mind that anybody could think Clare particularly attractive. 'You don't really mean that you think Clare is—'

'Not a bit of it. Shouldn't have said anything of the sort, schoolboy sense of humour, it's got me into trouble before. Still, I expect you'd like to get home a bit more often.' He leaned over the table. 'GBD might make it possible.'

'What?'

'I'll lay it on the line. We're interested in acquiring firms that are going concerns but aren't, how shall I put it, flourishing quite as they were. That doesn't matter, positive advantage in fact. Don't ask me why, it's one of these financial fiddles about stock distribution, I don't understand it except that after every little takeover the directors get richer on paper. Well, Lektreks sounds like a

95

candidate to me.'

'For take-over?'

'Hardly that, old boy. Not much to take over, is there? It would be acquisition, absorption, call it what you like. Where do you come in, you ask? No taste in nothing, we all know that.' He showed his teeth. 'This is all unofficial, you understand, but I think you'd get a parcel of stock in GBD.'

'I should?'

'And then, this is my own idea entirely, but I think we'd like to put you on the payroll. That glass cleaning device was damned clever. I know it didn't work out, but perhaps the next one will.' It was strange to have repeated to him the things he had told himself for years as consolation. Surely this was all too good to be true? Elsom's next words made this plain. 'The boys with slide rules.'

'I'm sorry, I didn't quite hear that.'

'I said, talking about terms, the boys with slide rules will settle all that.'

Arthur was unused to such terminology. 'I don't understand.'

'Accountants. We all have to do what they tell us, more's the pity. They come in, look at the books, fix a price. You can use your own chaps of course, but GBD will give you a square deal.'

'I see.' And he should have seen at once, should have known that it was impossible. The accountants would report that Lektreks did only a few thousand pounds' worth of business a year, and was worth almost nothing. When their report came through Elsom would see it and wonder where Arthur Brownjohn got his money. A whole trail of inquiry would be set up. GBD was not a promise but a menace. 'I shall have to think about it.'

'Do that. I think you'll find it will be to everybody's advantage.'

Elsom insisted on walking back to the office with him, telling him what a splendid outfit GBD was, and saying that independence was a wonderful thing and it was a shame the little man was going to the wall, but you couldn't hold out against the winds of change for ever. He left with protestations of goodwill and an assurance of not losing touch. Back in the office Arthur slumped in his chair and gave himself up to total gloom. Elsom was a fool, no doubt, look at the way he'd talked about Clare having a lover, but he was the kind of fool who didn't easily let go of an idea once he had hold of it. He had managed to conceal the Camb volume when Elsom came in and now he put it back on the shelf and took down a book in which he never failed to take delight, the account of the Wallace case. The beautifully logical complication of its structure somehow resembled music or chess. Wallace, a Liverpool insurance agent, had been accused of murdering his wife. His defence was an alibi based upon a telephone call from a man

97

named Qualtrough which had taken him wandering round Liverpool in search of a non-existent address. Had Wallace made the call himself and murdered his wife after stripping naked, as the prosecution suggested, or did Qualtrough really exist, was he the pseudonym of a shadowy figure thus dimly and momentarily seen, who then disappeared for ever?

He felt his eyes closing, and remembered that he had drunk half a bottle of wine. And then something jerked open his lids as though he had been given a small electric shock. The nerve ends of his body seemed to be tingling. Two completely separate ideas had come together in his mind. Major Easonby Mellon had to disappear. Clare also had to disappear. Why should they not run away together? Clare was thought by Elsom to be the kind of woman who might conceivably take a lover. In fact Clare would be dead, and her body would be buried in some conveniently undiscoverable spot, but it would seem that she was having an affair with Mellon and had gone off with him. There would be letters left to prove it. And the beauty of the idea was that Easonby was no Qualtrough, no mere name without a body. When the police investigated him they would find that he had an office, a business, a wife and a home. His existence was as real as that of Arthur Brownjohn.

That was the beginning of the idea. He

thought about it with rising excitement that afternoon and all the next day. Its prime requisite, of course, was the creation of a relationship, in fact a love affair, between Easonby Mellon and Clare. He bought a copy of *The Man Who Never Was*, which told the story of the deliberate creation during the war of a non-existent character, supported by all sorts of documents. Its use had been to deceive the Germans, Easonby Mellon's function here would be to deceive the police, and he had one immense advantage over the organisers of that realistic spoof, in the sense that Mellon was an established figure. On the other hand, there were difficulties which the secret service had not encountered.

The first of them was the question of Clare running away with the man. When a wife disappears, even though she may only have gone off for a week's holiday, her husband is likely to be suspected of killing her. How, to put it crudely, was her body to be disposed of? He did not drive a car, and he really could not imagine himself digging a hole in the garden and staggering out at night with a great wrapped bundle, even had such a procedure seemed judicious. To hide it inside the house or to dig up the garage floor would be dangerous as well as uncongenial. After a day's thought he gave up the elopement and decided on a bolder course. Clare's body should be discovered. She must be seen quite plainly to be a murder victim, and her murderer must be seen just as clearly to be Easonby Mellon.

Other problems to be solved, or relationships to be established, occurred to him. The project filled his mind completely. He jotted them down under three headings:

(1) Eliminate any link between E.M. and A.B.

(2) Establish relationship of E.M. and C.B. over period of time. First met in childhood?

(3) Decide precisely how project to be accomplished. E.M. is to be wiped out. How?

Under these main headings he made a number of notes. When he was sure that he had absorbed what was in the notes he burned them. The burning was a kind of smoke signal. It was time for action.

CHAPTER NINE

PREPARATIONS

May became June, and this was a fine June. The days were sunny, the nights mild. In the second week of the month he walked often in the Green Park, entering it from Piccadilly and then going through to Buckingham Palace, where he stared at the soldiers on duty as though they might have answers for some of the questions that still bothered him. On the way back he looked at the young couples who walked along oblivious of other people, like solicitor and client in consultation. He often had a feeling of isolation, sometimes doubted his own identity. He did not put it to himself in quite that way but the thought disturbed him, and once, when he was looking at the letters and postal orders for Matrimonial Assistance he asked aloud: 'What am I like then? What am I really like?' He was inorgiastic with Joan. He attributed this to the shock of discovering Pat Parker's treachery and this was in a way consoling, but at times it seemed to him that his hold on existence itself was failing. Who was he trying to protect? Did he want to live out the rest of his days as Arthur Brownjohn?

From such vague depressing thoughts he was roused by the need for ingenuity and for action. When Easonby Mellon disappeared there must be nothing left that could possibly connect him with Arthur Brownjohn, and this meant that his fingerprints must be eliminated both from Mellon's office and from the Clapham flat, in case some inquiring police officer noticed that the two were identical. This created a further problem because some prints must be left, at least in the office. How were they to be obtained?

He investigated the forgery of fingerprints. He found with pleasure that several methods were open to him. He could photograph a print in a book, have a rubber stamp made from the photograph, hold the stamp in his hand to impregnate it with body sweat, and thus leave impressions of the stamp in suitable places. Or he could have a print copied on to latex and glued to rubber gloves, using the gloves to leave prints. These methods had their dangers, however, since he would have to employ somebody to make the stamp or to have the prints copied, and he settled finally on a third method, involving the use of cellulose tape. He went out and bought a soapstone statuette of Buddha ('soapstone,' said one of the books he consulted, 'is an excellent print-taking surface.') He admired but did not touch it himself, and the dealer held the statuette firmly while extolling its beauty. Afterwards he was in agony while the man was wrapping it in tissue. Supposing the prints were destroyed! They survived, however, and on the following day he bought a pair of rubber gloves and completely cleaned the office. He paid particular attention to everything on the desk, the chair and the files, but he did not forget the door handle, the window sill, and other places likely to bear traces of prints.

Then came the ticklish part of the operation, the 'lifting' of the prints on the statuette. He used for this purpose a roll of cellulose tape. By rolling this tape gently over the Buddha he obtained a number of reasonably good prints. The last part of the process involved pressing the tape on to the best print-taking surfaces he could find on his desk and the filing cabinet. These 'roll-ons' (a technical term which he had used in his own mind) became fainter with use, but he managed to take a few more which he dotted about the room. These were the presumptive fingerprints of Easonby Mellon. They were not likely to deceive any serious police examination with a hand-lens, but the beauty of the device was that in his particular case this was all to the good. 'Ah ha,' the fingerprint expert would say, 'These prints are fakes. The man Mellon is obviously a criminal, trying to leave false prints.' And the joy of the whole thing was that he wanted them to think just this. When he had done with the statuette he sold it in the Portobello Road for less than a quarter of what it had cost him.

The problem of his prints at the Clapham flat was less easily solved. He considered and rejected one shocking idea, and decided that something was bound to occur to him in a day or two. In the meantime he had to provide Easonby Mellon with a background that was so far lamentably lacking. He took Joan to see a film called *The Eye of the Past*, of which he had read reviews. It was about a business executive who had risen to be the president of a corporation. Unknown to his friends he was the son of a convicted murderer, and had been prone to fits of uncontrollable rage in his youth. He was afraid that at some moment of crisis he would be moved to injure somebody because of the bad streak in his heredity, and his concern about this was shown in several dream sequences in which he was shown committing violent actions through a kind of fog which swirled about the screen. Sure enough his secret became known to a subordinate, a man who nursed a grudge about having been passed over for promotion. He now tried to obtain his ends by blackmail, and up to a point succeeded. The president paid him money, but when the man demanded promotion as well the president hit the man with a tyre lever, drove his car on to a rubbish dump, and set light to it. The body was identified, however, and the president was implicated because he had been seen leaving the dump. He fled to his home town, where he went to see an old nanny, who was the only person who had been kind to him when he was at home. In the end he was captured in her sitting-room, where she had given him the cookies he had loved in childhood. Under the influence of a long speech from her he gave himself up peacefully instead of fighting it out with the police.

'It was good,' Joan said afterwards. 'But very psychological. I mean, it couldn't really happen.'

He was sober, even grave. 'Something like it happened to me. My brother Chris went to prison. Robbery with violence. It killed our mother.'

'Go on.' Her mouth was agape. 'You never told me. Where was that?'

'In Canada. I left home when I was sixteen. Cut myself off.'

'You don't have any accent.'

'It was a long time ago. I've often thought that was the thing that made me go into the Service. I've been alone ever since.'

'E, you've got me.' Joan threw herself into his arms. She had been making coffee, and the milk boiled over.

In bed later on he said, 'Sometimes I read about Chris. Not Chris Mellon, that was just a name I took. He's always in and out of prison. And I know I've got the same thing in me. Violence. I could be violent.'

She shivered delicately. 'Well, you have been. That man you shot with the harpoon in Iceland.'

'That was in the way of work. I meant personally. If it came to the point I'd use violence.'

She shivered again and held him close. He thought it was a conversation she would remember.

On the following day Major Easonby Mellon visited Weybridge. He wore a green tweed suit which contrasted markedly with his hair. He ate lunch at a good hotel, where he made himself unpopular by loud unfavourable comments on the food and service and then by questioning his bill. He asked the hotel porter, as he had already asked two publicans, if he could recommend a really discreet place. Such a hotel is not easily found in the respectable commuter land of Weybridge but eventually he was told that the Embassy, by the river, might be the sort of place he was looking for. The reception clerk proved to be a bored young man who booked without question a double room for the following Wednesday.

'Just the one night, sir?'

'Not sure we shall stay the night. I'll pay for it, of course. May have to get back to London in the evening.' The clerk nodded. He hammered the point home. 'Been meeting elsewhere, you understand. Had to change because of damned snoopers. Must have discretion.'

'I understand.'

He paid for the room in advance and returned to London well satisfied.

The most difficult part of this phase in the operation remained, and he proposed to take the daring step of using Pat Parker to help in it. When Parker came in to the office he broached the matter. Parker was not in a good temper. The names they had taken from the files had almost all proved to be duds. One of the elderly gentlemen with an independent income had proved to be a retired dustman, and another was a widower at Bournemouth who was anxious to see something of London's famous night life. Others had written mere filth. There was only one possible mark, Parker said indignantly.

The Major shrugged. 'You chose the names.'

'You mean you'd have picked different ones.'

'Perhaps. After a time you get to know who's serious.'

'You'd better find a few serious ones. Otherwise we'll go back to the twenty a week, you wouldn't like that, would you?'

'How would Pat like to earn twenty-five pounds next Wednesday?'

Parker was smoking one of his cheroots. He took it from his mouth. 'For what?' When he was told he said suspiciously, 'What's the game?'

The Major hesitated, as though reluctant to confide. He saw Parker now with new eyes, a man of narrow vision who aspired to be nothing more than a petty crook living grubbily off a woman. In his new-found confidence he admitted that Pat would indirectly be helping him to nail a mark of his own. He did not go into details.

Parker was at sea. 'It's worth fifty.'

In the end they settled for forty, to be paid when the job had been done on the following Wednesday. Arthur Brownjohn travelled home in the train to Fraycut that Friday well pleased. In his brief-case were letters in Easonby

Mellon's erratic, dashing hand.

23 March

My dearest,
Next Wednesday then. Will it be like last Wed? You know it was marvellous, ecstasy, don't know how to say it. I love you, love seeing you in our little room. Sorry you thought it was dingy, but we have to be careful. Don't ask me about myself, can't tell you, too complicated, I've made silly mistakes, can't go back on them now. And you too? Is that what you meant when you talked about him?

E

2 April

Clare my darling,
Your body is white as the moon, your eyes are stars. If I were a poet I'd be able to write properly about it. After each meeting I feel more jealous of him and angry that he doesn't appreciate the treasures he's got. But I'm glad too, glad you don't belong to him because then you wouldn't belong utterly to me. I know you do.

Ever your devoted E

Dearest dearest C,
Dearest I was so upset, hurt and angry too—not angry for long, I never could be with you, but my anger when it comes is so intense it frightens me. What was there in my letters

that made you tear them up? Why is it wrong to wish we could be together always? Don't you know, dearest C, that I love you with every nerve and sinew in every possible way, mental and physical. I cannot bear to see you only once a week when you come to art class, it isn't enough. Why should you worry about him, whether you are deceiving him or not, it does not matter since you say he doesn't care. I don't understand your feelings. I have ties too, I told you that, but you know I will break them as soon as you say, so that we can be together. And we shall be together, we must, I cannot bear it otherwise and I cannot bear to think of him with you. I'm sorry my darling for writing like this. It is not just physical, it is everything. You are so cool and calm it exasperates me but you know I love you always.

E

There were a dozen letters altogether. He had composed them after careful study of the letters written by Edith Thompson to her lover Frederick Bywaters. Did they show obvious signs of their origin? Reading them through again with the attempted objectivity of an artist looking at his own work, he did not think so. Would it be possible for a handwriting expert to recognise Arthur Brownjohn's hand? A comparison with Mellon's correspondence would show they had been written by him.

Why should anyone seek to identify them with Arthur in view of that? Some of the sheets would have Clare's prints on them, even though they might be blurred, because they came from a packet of blue Basildon Bond paper that she had bought and handled before she took a dislike to the colour. They would not show Easonby Mellon's prints, but that could not be helped. He was pleased with the occasional irrelevancies he had put into the letters. 'Do you remember that day in the little tea shop at Sevenoaks ... you looked like raggy Maggie to-day but I loved you just the same ... rather worried in case Jamie recognised you ... you ask what we'll live on darling, we'll manage, lovers always do.' He was pleased also with the increasing hysteria of the letters' tone and the preoccupation which they showed with Arthur, referred to always as *him*. The last two or three letters were undated and the writing was much more erratic, to indicate excitement. It was obvious from them that Mellon had told her of his marriage and that Clare had refused to go away with him. His language became almost abusive:

I can't stand it and won't. *If I give up Joan why should you feel bound to* him, *what has he ever done to make you happy? You say I must not come down but I shall if I wish, why not, I am so wretched, what harm can it do, I would sooner come down and have it out once and for all.* I shall not give up because I love you *and if you do not love me any more I would sooner end everything.*

It was repetitive stuff to read, like all love letters, but it seemed convincing. At least, it convinced him.

CHAPTER TEN

FINISHING TOUCHES

DIARY
Friday June 13.

Friday the 13th, unlucky, rather worried. But it wasn't. Not that I am superstitious anyway, but you never know. Clare now quite usual self. Said she heard I'd seen Elsom. Yes, I said, had to be in London and he'd dropped in. His proposition sounded interesting but I'd have to investigate it, didn't want to lose my independence. She agreed, but wasn't interested. Why should I worry about that? But I do. Went on to talk about discussion in local Liberal Party. Man named Ffoliot-Jenkins says they are too much like Labour. Why should I have to listen to that, what does she take me for?

Saturday, June 14
Shopped in morning. Hubble called while

out, gave Clare clean bill of health. Later she went to Liberal committee. I talked to Susan, asked her if she had seen strange man around.

Susan What kind of man?

Self Reddish-brown beard, loud clothes.

S Don't know who you mean.

Self Yesterday I saw him leaving this house just before I came in.

S Better ask Mrs. Brownjohn about him.

Self I did. She didn't know what I was talking about.

S No more do I. Probably some sort of hawker and Mrs. Brownjohn didn't open the door.

Self He didn't look like a hawker.

I hugged *myself during this conversation.*
Susan doesn't like me, all to the good perhaps.
I think it sunk in, left her curious.

Sunday, June 15

Houses are built of single bricks joined with mortar. To-day went for drinks to the Paynes'. Had a chance to talk to Mrs. P, their daughter goes sometimes to Clare's art class at Weybridge. I asked what time she got back, Mrs. P said about 7 o'clock. I said that was funny, I'd rung Clare last two Wednesdays about 9.30, no reply. Mrs. P pricked up ears, didn't think Wendy came back with Clare (I knew she didn't, Clare can't stand her!) but would find out. No no, I said hurriedly, don't do that, probably the line was out of order. We agreed telephone service was terrible. She will ask her though. I let Mrs. P see I was worried, said it was a pity I couldn't be home more. Every little thing tells.

Monday, June 16

Why do I have to do it? To-day C came to me, said suddenly it was a pity I had to go away so much in mid-week, she missed me. I said she had the Liberal Party, art class, etc. 'Yes, but we could go out together. To the theatre perhaps. I haven't been to the theatre in years. Perhaps if Elsom—'

Perhaps, I said. Then she looked as if she was sorry for having spoken. 'You know I never interfere.'

Why do I have to do it, I wondered then? I felt sorry, but it's no use. Events have a logic. They must work themselves out. And what has C ever given me in the way of companionship or sex or money? Silly to be sentimental, but I am sometimes. Life is a terrible tangle. Why can't it be straightforward? To-day we gardened together. In the afternoon a new American car came. I had to adjust it before it fitted the slot, but then it worked marvellously. Raced it against several British cars, American won easily. Clare made milk jelly, horrible.

On Tuesday he was again in London. At Romany House the cares of Arthur Brownjohn were sloughed off from Major

113

Easonby Mellon. There were letters to be sent out, some introducing Patricia Parker, there were people to see. Then a quick, early lunch. Then Major Easonby Mellon went to Waterloo Station and took the train to Fraycut. Was it Easonby Mellon who took the train? In the carriage which he occupied alone, he considered the question. Could Arthur Brownjohn have done what he was going to do this afternoon? It was one thing to drop hints and make discreet suggestions, quite another to mount the frontal assault that was to be essayed now. No, Arthur could not have done it. But the hand of Easonby Mellon was firm, the smile with which he viewed himself in the carriage glass had about it a touch of bravado.

Arthur Brownjohn had never done more than say a timid good morning to the ticket collector, who looked remarkably like the comedian Phil Silvers. Major Mellon first handed him the wrong half of his ticket and then asked the way to a house called The Laurels.

Phil Silvers lacked patience. 'Never 'eard of it.' He turned away.

The Major bristled. 'Just keep a civil tongue in your head when you're asked a civil question.'

'I said *never 'eard of it.*'

'The Laurels, Livingstone Road.'

'Down the High Street, first left, second

114

right.'

The Major fumbled in his pocket, produced a shilling, handed it over, nodded, walked away. A sideways look revealed Phil Silvers looking after him with a stare that blended surprise and disdain.

Major Mellon sauntered up the High Street and went into the Catherine of Aragon, a pub which Arthur Brownjohn had never entered. He ordered a double whisky and asked the barmaid whether she knew The Laurels in Livingstone Road. He had received directions at the station, but couldn't find it.

The barmaid, by contrast with Phil Silvers, was made up of good humour. She laughed heartily. 'You're walking away from it.'

'Right about turn, is it?' The Major suited the action to the words, to the amusement of half a dozen regulars in the bar. 'Never had any sense of direction. Will you take a drop of something, my dear?'

The barmaid took a drop of gin and remarked, after the Major had had two more drinks, that he seemed to be in no hurry.

'In a manner of speaking I'm not. I'm not damn' well supposed to be here at all.'

'You're not?' Laughter rumbled in the barmaid, then became quiescent.

'I've come down to see a filthy rotten little skunk and tell him what I think of him, that's all.'

'And I bet you will, too. But don't go doing

anything you shouldn't. What's it about, a woman?' When he nodded she laughed, in relief at something so familiar. 'You know what they say, a woman's not worth it.'

'This particular lady is.' He took out silver, placed it on the counter. It was nearly three o'clock. The bar was almost empty. The barmaid poured another whisky and, in response to his imperious gesture, another gin for herself.

'You think a deal of her, don't you?' she said perspicaciously. 'What's this man done, then?'

'Nothing. I am in the wrong. I should not be here at all.' He added reflectively, 'I meant to purchase a weapon, but I refrained. I feared I should do someone an injury.'

'A weapon!' The laughter coiled back into her stomach, leaving a fat tense face. 'I'll have no weapons in my bar.'

'I said I haven't bought it. I shall try reason first.'

She opened the flap of the bar counter. 'Closing time.' As he walked out her speculative gaze followed him.

Ten minutes later he turned into Livingstone Road. This was the ticklish part of the operation. Clare was, or should be, at a Children's Care Committee. Susan was, or should be, working in the house. He walked past the front gate two or three times, apparently unobserved. Then the milkman

116

came along the road. The Major had his hand on the gate. He turned away, came face to face with the milkman, who gave him an incurious glance as he passed carrying milk and eggs. When the man had gone the Major returned, pushed open the gate, walked round the garden to the side of the house, picked up a handful of gravel and small stones from the garden path and threw them at the first floor bedroom window. There was a ping as the window cracked. From the bathroom window adjoining Susan's head peered. She shouted something that he could not hear. He shouted unintelligibly back and then left at a smart trot which slowed to a walk as he turned the corner of Livingstone Road. He caught a bus in the High Street which took him to Esher, and from Esher a train back to Waterloo.

DIARY
Thursday, June 19

Stone walls do not a prison make
Nor iron bars a cage.

Very true, that poem. Prisons are mental. It's as if you were enclosed in a room for ever with other people. I often feel I'd have more chance inside the stone walls of a prison. There you can cut through the bars and get out. In the room with other people you can't get out except by getting rid of them. Isn't there a play about all that?

Writing this in train on the way up to

Birmingham. All part of the plan.

Notes on progress. Contradiction here, have to admit it. I really like all the complications, pitting my wits against 'authority,' solving problems as they come up. I've done so much since Monday and it's all so clever, so well arranged, that I can't help being pleased with it. I said I'd never do anything, but I've proved myself wrong! Have to be careful, though. This liking for complication is my weakness.

Notes, then. Tuesday night bought the gun at a shop in Brixton which has lots of flick-knives in the window. Told the man I wanted it to protect house against burglars, had no licence. Paid through the nose for it, naturally. Smith and Wesson .38, same thing that American police use, the man said. Surprised it was so big. Unpleasant, don't like the look of the thing. Left it with Joan, said if Flexner reappeared show it to him. Seemed to regard it all as a game, extraordinary woman.

Then Wednesday. What a day! First arranged to go up to Birmingham to-day, A.M. *to see Gibson of Steel Alloys. Said I wanted to talk to him about whether he'd be interested in new lines I'd been offered by U.S. firm (True!). Then rang Elsom, arranged to look in and see him to-night about 6 o'clock. Then sent telegram to Clare saying meet me Waterloo Station 4 o'clock Wednesday. Point was to keep her away from Weybridge art class*

118

that afternoon. Thought of her waiting at Waterloo getting angry, hugged myself. Appealed to sense of humour, I must say. Then the tricky part of the operation which was not pleasant, taking Pat (Bitch) Parker to Weybridge. Was this a mistake, over-complication, should I have made some other arrangement? Still worried about it.

First she came to the office with the man. He asked again what it was all about. Said divorce case, that seemed to satisfy him. Then he demanded fifty pounds instead of the forty we'd fixed. Blackmail, but what could I do? Very angry, but no good showing it. Had to agree. At least she'd bought a good thick veil as I'd asked. Couldn't see features clearly behind it.

Got to Weybridge just after 3.30, signed register 'Mr. and Mrs. John Smith,' classical. Same desk clerk, gave him a fiver, ordered bottle of champagne in room. She perked up at that. Sent her into bathroom so that he shouldn't see her when he brought it up.

Then gave Miss Pat a real shock. As I opened the bottle, poured it, she said archly, 'What happens now?'

The bitch was ready for anything. She disgusted me. Took out a pack of cards, asked if she played bezique. 'You've brought me up here to play cards!' Didn't want to cause a scene, said this was strictly business. Glared at me. 'I always knew you were a creep.'

119

EM could have made a blistering reply, really given her the rough side of his tongue. Didn't do so, just said she was getting well paid for it. Didn't play, however, so played patience alone. She sat smoking, said I hadn't even brought bloody papers to read, called me a creep again. Sticks and stones, etc., but words will never hurt me.

At a quarter to six mussed up bed thoroughly, creasing sheets and denting pillows, while she stared at me. At six o'clock we left, she wearing veil. Looked at her figure as I walked out, stockier than I thought, really quite like Clare, especially legs. Travelled up together to Waterloo, not speaking. Gave her the other twenty-five pounds, took it without a thank-you. Good-bye Miss P (B) Parker.

Then to Clapham. Ought to write about that, but can't. Makes me shiver to think of what I had to do. It makes me angry to think I should have to work by such deceits. Why does society punish a man for going through a social form with two different women? And if all the things said about the sacrament of marriage, one flesh, etc. are true, why should a wife be allowed a separate bank account? Absurd. The habits by which we live and think are not what we believe.

Only writing this to avoid saying anything about last night and Joan. Ashamed, I don't know why.

120

It was those hours of Wednesday evening that he fought to eliminate from his mind afterwards. Recollection of them brought terror to him for he knew that what he did, even though it had been forced on him, was wrong.

Seven-thirty. He opened the door, Joan greeted him. He met her with a deliberate brightness that oppressed him by its falsity. 'We're going out.'

'Out?'

'The flicks. *La Ronde* is on at the Globe, you've always wanted to see it.'

'But E, I've got some nice chops I was just going to grill.'

'No time for that, my girl. *La Ronde*, it's—' He kissed the tips of her fingers. 'Anton Walbrook.'

'I know, but.' She did not complete the sentence, peered at him. 'Something's wrong.'

'Nothing. Don't be absurd.'

'It's to do with the Department, that man coming. You're going to leave me, E, I know you are.'

The image crossed his mind of a bitch knowing that it is going to be put down. Why should he feel like this, when he was doing nothing to hurt her? She clung to him. 'You don't love me any more.'

'Yes, yes.'

'I love you, E. If I didn't have you, there'd be nothing left, I should kill myself.' To this he made no reply. 'Come to bed. Now.'

He removed her arms from his neck. 'You said the Tallises are away?' They were the occupants of the other maisonette in the house.

She stared. 'You want to get me out of the house?'

In your own interest, he said to himself, while aloud he told her not to talk nonsense, he was coming with her. The stresses of the day had overcome him. He felt as if he were running a high temperature, and when he put his hand to his forehead it was covered with sweat. In the end she agreed to go, but insisted that he come with her while she put on her coat. When they were outside the house she said abruptly, 'The garden shed.'

'Yes?'

'Why is it locked? What have you done with the key?'

He did not answer, but wrenched her arm so that she cried out. The night was hot. He could feel the sweat rolling down his body, dropping from the torso and pouring down his legs. His collar was wringing wet. Involuntarily he looked down to see whether water was staining his shoes. He swayed, and she caught his arm. 'What is it?'

'Nothing.'

They crossed the road and walked along

122

beside the common. The scent of grass was strong in his nostrils, the roar of traffic exceptionally loud. Suddenly the grass scent was replaced by that of petrol, moving over him in sickly waves. The gears of a lorry grated, and the sound broke on his ears like a shriek of pain. In a field boys played cricket, the ball thudding on bat like a drum. Was it the traffic noise or something wrong with his hearing that made the words she was saying merge into indistinguishable blobs of sound? He turned his head to speak, but she shrieked something and made a gesture. He turned back. Slowly, as it seemed slowly, a cricket ball, reddish brown, moved through the blue air. A long way back on the field the players all stood turned towards him, a theatre audience waiting for something to happen. Joan was calling out, he moved his head, the ball went past (with a super-sensitivity of hearing that replaced his deafness he heard it pass, making a distinct train-like whistle). Then it was in the road and had banged against the tinny side of a car.

'That almost hit you.' Her voice sounded faint now, as though wax were in his ears. He shook his head and smiled slightly. A man picked up the ball and threw it back to the cricketers.

The cinema was half-empty. They sat in a row with only two other people in it. They arrived near the end of the first scene, the

123

soldier's encounter with the prostitute. The darkness surrounding them seemed to have something physical about it, like a blanket. He was jerked sharply into attention by a new theme in the music, and turned to look at Joan. She was staring straight ahead at the screen, and in profile her face had a crumpled, folded expression. Tears crawled like snailmarks down her cheek and she made no attempt to wipe them away.

This dumb-animal misery was too much for him. The day had been so full of anxiety and there was still so much to do, including what lay ahead of him that evening, that he was incapable of making the consoling gesture she needed. He closed his eyes against the images on the screen which mocked his own situation, and let the music flow over him. Within his head there moved incoherent abstract forms. Bright lights converged, met and noiselessly exploded, to be replaced by waves of sound and colour moving restlessly like the sea. They gave way to pictures of people—Pat Parker was there with a veil thickly covering her face. He removed it to find another veil which he pulled aside, and another and another. The important thing was seeing and touching, to assure himself that it was Pat and not somebody else who had come with him to Weybridge. When he touched her hand he knew that something was wrong.

He opened his eyes. The screen was in front

of him, figures moved across it as they should do. What was wrong? He looked down to see Joan's hand inside his trousers, felt the desperate groping of her fingers which moved as if she were trying to bring back the dead to life. She was still staring at the screen, and her hand might have been an agent remote from the rest of her body. He removed the hand, buttoned his trousers, stood up. She clutched his arm. He whispered: 'Got to make a phone call, back in five minutes,' walked up the aisle and out of the cinema. Less than half an hour had passed since they entered.

And less than half an hour after that he had done the thing that terrified him. He spent the night in a London hotel. In the morning, before taking the train to Birmingham, he read the papers carefully. Two of them reported the incident. 'Mystery Fire at Clapham. Arson Suspected.' Number 48 Elm Drive had been gutted, and people had been evacuated from Number 50. Nobody had been hurt. An empty petrol tin had been found and also some cotton waste in the garden shed belonging to the house. Arson was suspected.

He shivered as he read. It had gone as he intended, with no damage to anybody except an insurance company, yet he still felt uneasy. The crime against property seemed in a way to be a crime against himself. But it had been effective. There would be no personal trace left at Clapham of Major Easonby Mellon.

CHAPTER ELEVEN

THE ACT

He had not decided upon the method and manner of committing the act without thought. It was tempting to play with the idea of planning some deliberate deception about the time of death. 'It is not possible to be certain about the rate of cooling of a body': those encouraging words had been written by no less a medico-legal expert than Sir Sydney Smith, and books of medical jurisprudence all spoke with delightful uncertainty about establishing the precise time of death. Suppose that one placed an electric fire near to a body, the time of death would appear to be an hour or two later than was actually the case. Or suppose— more ingenious and interesting—that one took ice cubes from the refrigerator and placed them in plastic non-leaking containers at various points about the body, the normal cooling process should be speeded up. He reluctantly rejected such ideas, partly because of the distaste that he felt for having anything to do with a dead body, but chiefly (or so he felt) because such ingenuity was in itself to be deprecated. If the police happened to notice that the electric fire, although turned off, was still curiously warm, if ice water somehow leaked out of the plastic packs, if in fact the police thought that deliberate deception was being attempted, might they not immediately suspect him? The strength of his position was that Arthur Brownjohn and Easonby Mellon were two wholly separate characters, and that there was no reason in the world why they should be associated. This was what he must remember. The act should be simple, quick and obvious. His plan was simple, and entailed practically no risk.

At Euston Station, on his return from Birmingham he telephoned Clare, and cut short a burst of recriminatory phrases by saying that he was coming home and wanted to see her.

There must have been something strange in his tone, for she checked abruptly as a horse coming to a jump. 'What about?'

'I can't explain now, but—'

'You can't explain,' she said incredulously.

'You're alone, aren't you?'

'Of course I am alone. I am just finishing my lunch.'

'I shall be back soon. Don't tell anybody I'm coming, will you?'

'Arthur, have you been drinking?'

'I'll be there soon after three.' He put down the telephone. His hand was shaking.

In the station lavatory he changed into Easonby Mellon's clothes, and carefully adjusted the wig and beard. He went out carrying Arthur Brownjohn's clothes and diary in his suitcase. He caught the two-thirty train from Waterloo for the half-hour journey to Fraycut.

This time Major Mellon made his way straight out of the station in the direction of Livingstone Road. Phil Silvers was not on duty, and the man at the barrier took his ticket without a glance. The Laurels stood foursquare in exurban dignity. The rest of Livingstone Road appeared to sleep. He opened the gate, which gave its accustomed small squeak, walked up the path, inserted the key in the lock, turned it, was inside. Mr. Slattery stared at him accusingly, as though aware of the revolver in his jacket pocket. The door of the living-room opened, and Clare came out. 'What—' she said, and stopped. He found himself holding his breath, as if something important depended on her words. Then she completed the sentence.

'What are you doing in those ridiculous clothes, and that—' She seemed to find it impossible to specify the wig and beard. 'Take it all off immediately.'

She had known him at once. It was awful. His fists were clenched into tight balls. 'I can explain.'

'Your telegram, what was the meaning of that? I waited for more than an hour at Waterloo. And now this fancy dress.'

'I said I could explain.'

128

'I doubt it very much. I cannot think what possible explanation there can be.'

He heard himself saying that it was quite simple, and knew with dismay that the tones were those of Arthur Brownjohn, not of Easonby Mellon. How could boldness have so speedily and humiliatingly abandoned him? One hand went into a pocket and drew out the revolver.

'What is the *meaning* of this masquerade?' Clare was becoming angry, it could be seen in the thickening of her neck muscles and the spot of colour in her cheeks. He was near the door of the living-room and she stood in the middle of it just beside the mottled grey sofa. She saw what was in his hand, and her reaction was one of pure exasperation. She spoke like a mother to a misbehaving child. 'Arthur, what are you doing? Put it *down*.'

'No.' He found it impossible to speak, then swallowed and managed it. 'I really must explain.'

She took a step towards him. He retreated. 'If you could see how silly you look.'

'Silly!' he cried out. The word moved him to anger. He raised the revolver, squeezed the trigger. Nothing happened.

'Of course you do. Just get that stuff off and wash your face and you'll feel better.'

'I am not silly,' he shouted. Why didn't she realise that he was a dangerous man? He realised that he had not moved the safety catch and did so. Suddenly the revolver went off, making a tremendous noise. The kickback jolted his arm severely. What had happened to the bullet? He became aware that Clare was strangely pale.

She took another step towards him and said in a low voice, 'What is the matter with you, Arthur?'

He retreated. He had his back to the door. The revolver went off again, almost deafening him. This time she put her hands to her stomach, so evidently the bullet had hit her, but she did not fall down. Instead she put out a hand, and he felt that if she succeeded in touching him something terrible would happen. He cried out something, he could not have said what, and fired again and again, he did not know how many times or where the bullets went. There was a ping of glass and he thought: 'Heavens, I've broken the french window.' He looked and saw the window starred at one point, and with a deep crack down the centre. He was so much distressed by this time that his attention was temporarily distracted from Clare. He saw, however, that she was badly hurt. She appeared to be trying to speak to him, but failed to do so. Blood shot in a stream from her mouth—he jumped back hurriedly so that it should not touch him—and she fell over the back of the sofa and then down the side of it to the floor, clawing at the sofa for support and making unintelligible noises in her throat. She seemed still to be trying to say something to him, but he could not imagine what it was. She lay on the carpet groaning. Blood continued to trickle from her mouth. He found it unendurable that she was not dead, perhaps would not die. The revolver was empty, but in any case he could not have fired it again. He stood and watched helplessly as she tried to inch her way across the carpet to—what would it be?—of course, the telephone. There was blood on her face now, and she moved more slowly. He could not have said whether it was seconds or minutes before he realised that she was not moving at all.

It would have been impossible for him to touch her with his gloved hands, but he moved across with the caution he would have used in approaching a squashed but possibly still dangerous insect, and rolled her over with his foot. She lay still, staring at the ceiling with her eyes open. She was, she must be, dead.

He felt that he could no longer bear to be in the house. He dropped the revolver to the floor, looked round him without seeing anything, and ran out of the room. His case stood in the hall. He picked it up, opened the front door, and began to run down the path. Then he checked himself. In the garden of Endholme old Mr. Lillicrapp was at work with his fork and trowel. He straightened up and said, 'Afternoon. Some boys been breaking windows round here. Heard the glass go. Thought it might be mine, but it wasn't. Not next door, I hope.' He laughed heartily, but the man leaving The Laurels in a hurry made no reply. Mr. Lillicrapp leaned on his fork and stood looking after the man as he walked down the road. Discourtesy was rampant nowadays. He ascribed it less to rudeness than to the hurry and bustle of modern life.

PART TWO

AFTER THE ACT

CHAPTER ONE

DISCOVERY

Major Easonby Mellon died in a train lavatory somewhere between Fraycut and Waterloo. The clothes, wig and beard that had been the corporeal marks of his existence went into the suitcase. The police, when they checked, might find that Mellon had got on to the train at Fraycut. From that point onwards he would have vanished. They would check at Waterloo and at the intermediate stations, and would find no trace of him. Arthur Brownjohn, a man totally inconspicuous except for the bald head concealed by a trilby hat, got off the train at Waterloo, deposited a suitcase in the Left Luggage office, and put the ticket carefully into his wallet. He spent a few minutes in the buffet and then bought a ticket and caught the next train to Fraycut. He walked from the station to Elsom's house, which was ten minutes' distance from his own.

The Elsoms lived in a new development of what were called superior town houses, and he was happy to feel that the man who walked up their short drive and rang their three-tone chiming bell, was in complete command of himself. The revulsion he had felt during and after the act remained, but the terror

135

accompanying it had vanished when he shed the appurtenances of Easonby Mellon in the lavatory. Waiting at Fraycut Station, as he had had to do because the train was late, he had been dreadfully agitated. The fear had possessed him that a policeman would come up and say, 'You were seen leaving The Laurels a few minutes ago under suspicious circumstances, and I must ask you to accompany me to the police station.' When he became Arthur Brownjohn again he shrugged off these fears, and indeed was able to see that everything had happened for the best. That Mr. Lillicrapp had seen the murderer leaving, and that he should have displayed such obvious agitation on the station platform, must surely remove any doubt that might linger in the official mind. If he had planned all that— and it was with a shade of reluctance that he acknowledged what had happened as unplanned and at the time distressing—it could not have worked out better. The call on Elsom was a precautionary measure designed to show that at (he looked at his watch) six o'clock he had been perfectly calm. And he congratulated himself that he had passed the test, that he *was* calm. Many men, after all, would not have been. It was with insouciance that, as the door opened, he faced Elsom's fine teeth.

'What a very nice place you have here.' In fact he detested the appearance of the living-room, the picture window, the differently-coloured walls, the rugs placed with careful carelessness on the wood block floor, the absence of a fire-place. How could you possibly call such a place a home?

'We like it. Melissa's done the furnishing. She's got taste.' All Elsom's statements were positive. They both invited contradiction and implied that it would not be tolerated. Melissa, a wispy blonde with a tiny triangular face, came in and said that she was sorry.

'I beg your pardon?'

'Melissa couldn't get along to your party. She had one of her heads.'

'One of my heads.' A red-tipped claw was placed upon the longest side of the triangle, the forehead. 'I believe your wife has heads.'

'What? Oh yes, she does have heads.' The conversation was proving less easy to maintain than he had expected. An image flashed across his mind of Clare with two heads. He rejected this, and it was succeeded by one of her face as he had last seen it, with blood trickling down the chin.

'I find the only thing is a darkened room. Does your wife find that too?'

He began to wish that he were alone with Elsom. However, it proved that Melissa had come in only to make polite conversation. She extolled the virtues of the new development, said how pleasant it was to be among people who were really your sort, expressed a hope that she would meet Clare very soon, and drifted delicately from the room.

'She's very sensitive.' Elsom closed the door decisively. 'What'll it be, gin, whisky, vodka, sherry? You name it, we have it.'

'A little vodka.' He coughed. 'I believe that has no smell. I mustn't go home smelling of drink.'

'Clare wouldn't like it, eh?'

'The truth is, I must confess, I have rather a weak head.'

'You haven't been home yet?'

'I came straight from London. I wanted to see you.'

'Here I am. Anything I can straighten out, be happy to do it.' Elsom settled himself in an oddly-shaped chair. 'Fire away.'

'The truth is Lektreks hasn't been doing very well lately. In the last couple of years, I mean.' Elsom's brisk nod showed him to be unsurprised. 'And Clare is not very keen on my giving up.'

'Doesn't want you round the house all day.' Elsom guffawed, gulped at his drink. 'So?'

He said carefully, 'It might be a question of what terms you have in mind.'

'I told you, that's in the hands of the slide rule boys. But I've never known anyone who dealt with GBD who had any complaints afterwards.'

'You did say you might employ me. My inventions.'

138

'Your inventions, yes.' Elsom was obviously about to launch on a long speech, and Arthur took the chance to look surreptitiously at his watch. Just after half past six. How long should he go on with this, when could he decently leave, having established the fact of his calmness and coherence? He listened for what seemed like minutes to Elsom circuitously conveying that what really interested GBD was Lektreks and that the offer of a job was conditional on the purchase of the firm. He nodded occasionally, and was astonished to find that his eyelids had actually closed for a moment. He jerked into attention at mention of Clare's name.

'Why not give her a ring?' Elsom leaned forward doggily in his chair, ready to spring.

'Give Clare a ring?'

'Unless you've any more problems, conference is finished, agreed? Why not ask her round for a drink, Melissa would love to meet her, won't take a couple of minutes in the car.'

'We haven't got a car.'

'Shanks's pony then, it's a fine evening. Or I'll nip round and fetch her.'

Why not, he suddenly agreed with doggish Elsom, why not give Clare a ring? There was something gruesome about the thought of the telephone ringing in the empty house, the body on the floor with blood coming out of the mouth, but it was necessary not to think of that. You must be brave, he told himself, you must not draw back now. He saw the sequence of events, the telephone call, no reply, where can Clare have got to, must get back at once, no doubt she's just slipped out for a few minutes but still. Perhaps Elsom would drive him back. If he did, so much the better.

'Very good idea. I'll ring her now if I may use your phone.'

The telephone was in a corner of the room, beneath a grinning mask. As he picked it up and dialled he saw with extreme vividness the telephone at the house. It stood in the hall, an old-fashioned black instrument, different in colour and even in shape from the red telephone in his hand. Burr-burr, the telephone said in his ear, burr-burr. It would take Clare four burr-burrs to get there from the living-room, a dozen from upstairs. He would give it something over a dozen before turning to Elsom, brows knit together, to say that there seemed to be no reply.

The burr-burr stopped. A man's voice said, 'Yes?'

He thought for a moment that he would drop the telephone. Then he managed to say, 'What number is that? Who is it?'

The number was his own. The speaker did not give his identity.

'I want to speak to my wife. Mrs. Brownjohn. Call her to the telephone, please. And who is that?'

'Just a moment.'

In the next seconds he expected to hear Clare's voice and to be assured that nothing had happened, the whole thing had been something merely imagined in his diary. A different man's voice said, 'Mr. Brownjohn?'

'Yes. Who are you? Where is my wife?'

'Coverdale, sir. Detective-Inspector, C.I.D. I've got some bad news for you.'

He did not have to make his voice quaver as he asked the nature of the news, and was told it. How had the police got there so quickly? Was there something threatening in the Inspector's voice? He was asked where he was.

'A friend's house. Very near.'

'Give me the address, sir. I'll send round a car.'

He put down the telephone for a moment. 'Not bad news, I hope,' Elsom asked eagerly.

'The address, what's the address?'

'I don't get you. What address?'

'The address *here*, you fool.' The actions and emotions of the day were too much for him, and he began to weep. Elsom looked at him appalled, called his wife, and then picked up the telephone. Even in the grip of the hysteria which was not checked by the huge drink Melissa poured for him, he could not help noticing the businesslike way in which Elsom received the news, opening his jacket to reveal a battery of pens and pencils and selecting one with which to make notes. He

141

chose a ballpoint which wrote in red, and as Arthur remembered the trickle of blood, this seemed to him absurd. The tears streaming down his cheeks became tears of laughter. He made a gesture at the ballpoint, and the laughter grew higher. Elsom put down the telephone, turned, said, 'Sorry about this.' He saw nothing, but felt a tremendously hard blow on the jaw, one that rattled his teeth and knocked him off the chair arm on which he had been sitting, on to the carpet.

Melissa's triangular face bent anxiously over him. He looked up, unable to focus properly. 'Oh, Derek,' she said, 'I hope you haven't hit him too hard.'

CHAPTER TWO

CONVERSATION WITH COVERDALE

Everything seemed to be happening at once, and everybody treated him with a totally agreeable care and delicacy. When the police car arrived he was still on the sofa, with Melissa holding a damp towel to his jaw and Elsom full of apologies for not knowing his own strength. Then into the car—it was the first time he had ever been in a police car, and he said so to the detectives—and in a flash they were back at The Laurels. He was still feeling shaky, and entered the house holding the arm of one of the detectives.

In the hall Mr. Slattery gave him his customary look, but otherwise everything was changed. As always happens when the police enter a house where a violent event has occurred, the whole place seemed to have been taken over by them. There were cars outside the house, men dashed in and out carrying bits of equipment, and they talked to each other briskly. 'Got all you want? . . . Is Jerry at the station . . . Finished the downstairs and the hall, trying upstairs.' Feet clattered in and out, up and down. He tried to look in the living-room, but was not allowed to do so. A man appeared, nodded, said 'Mr. Brownjohn, come along.' Where were they going? It proved to be the kitchen. Clare wouldn't like this, he thought as they sat in chairs on opposite sides of the kitchen table, she wouldn't like it at all.

'My name's Coverdale.' He was a big man with a lumpy, knobbly face and a bulky body that seemed to be straining out of his shiny blue suit. 'Sergeant Amies.' Startled, Arthur looked round and saw another man beside the door. 'Cigarette?'

'Thank you, I don't smoke.'

Coverdale lighted one himself, staring across the table all the while. Was it the prelude to a fierce interrogation? Instead he said, 'Put the kettle on, Bill. Mr. Brownjohn

143

could do with a cuppa. You've had a shock.'

'Yes.'

'Stands to reason it was a shock.'

'I was a little hysterical. A friend had to hit me.'

'He made a job of it. You're going to have a nice little lump.'

'I don't really know what's happened.'

'Stupid. Course you don't.' Was he guileful, or as straightforward as he appeared? 'Somebody broke in, that's the way it looks at the moment, burglar perhaps. Your wife surprised him.'

'She—she is dead?'

'I'm afraid so. I told you on the telephone.'

'Yes. Somehow it's hard to believe.' This was true. Clare's presence seemed to him to hang like a gas cloud over the whole house.

'You need that cup of tea.'

'Tea coming up.' The Sergeant poured it into mugs instead of the cups Clare would have used. The tea itself was strong and sweet, and he did feel better after drinking it.

'Amateur,' the Inspector said.

'What?'

'If it was done that way, somebody breaking and entering and then your wife surprising him, it was an amateur. Pros don't carry guns.'

'She was shot?'

'Didn't I say?' It was the first hint that guile might lurk behind the blue marble eyes. 'Emptied the revolver in a panic, fired all over the place. Amateur sure enough.'

What was the best question to ask? 'When did it happen?'

'Round about three-thirty.'

'I don't think that's right.' Surprise showed on Coverdale's lumpy face. 'I mean Clare has—had—rather fixed habits, for being in and for being out. She was almost always in on Friday afternoons. So it's not likely she would have come back and surprised a burglar. I mean, she would have been here.'

'Interesting.' Coverdale drained his cup. 'Eh, Amies?'

'Interesting.' The Sergeant whisked away the cups, began to wash them up.

'You think it was personal, some enemy?'

'Oh, I didn't say that.'

'You got any enemies, your wife got any?'

'No. Nobody who would do this.'

'Happily married? No quarrels?'

'Certainly not.' He was genuinely shocked by the suggestion. 'We were quite happy. My work takes me away from home rather a lot. Clare had developed interests of her own. I was pleased about that, but I suppose in a way they tended to separate us.'

'Tried to ring you this afternoon.' Coverdale's voice was casual. 'Your office. No reply.'

'It's a small office, just an address. I don't have a secretary.'

Silence. Amies turned from the sink. 'Going

to ask him, sir?'

'May as well.' He could feel his legs trembling. 'Any idea where you were this afternoon around three-thirty?'

'I went up to Birmingham this morning to see a client. I caught the two-fifteen back. I was in the train from Birmingham to London.'

'Mind telling us the client's name?' That was Amies again.

'Steel Alloys Limited. I saw Mr. Gibson, left him soon after twelve, had lunch—'

'Mind telling us where?'

'A pub called the Dog and Duck, just off the Bull Ring. I got in to Euston—oh, I can't remember, but not before half past three.'

'They're not that quick yet, are they?' Coverdale laughed heartily.

'I don't understand why you're asking me these questions.'

'Shouldn't have done perhaps. Don't want to upset you. Leave it until to-morrow if you like.' Coverdale got up. 'Like us to fix a hotel for you? Don't suppose you'll want to stay here, wouldn't advise it anyway.' Amies had washed up the cups. The two men moved to the door. He felt a passionate reluctance to let them go.

'There was a question I wanted to ask you.'

'Yes?'

A man put his head round the kitchen door, muttered something to Amies, who went out. Coverdale looked inquiring.

146

'How do you know it was half past three when it happened?'

'Your next door neighbour, name's Lillicrapp. Heard some glass breaking, saw a man run out of your house and down the road. Went round the back to have a look. The glass was your french window, broken by one of the shots. He looked through the window, saw your wife on the floor, rang us straight away. That's the sort of co-operation we like to get from the public.'

'This man he saw. You've got a description?'

Coverdale nodded. The door opened again, Amies said, 'Spare a minute, sir?'

He was left alone in the kitchen. His existence with Clare surrounded him. The plates had their own place on the dresser shelves and she had been especially pleased by the mats beside them, a series called 'Cries of Old London' which she had bought only a few months ago. Attached to the gas cooker was an automatic lighter which he had bought for her. He sat at the kitchen table and put his head in his hands. His jaw ached.

'Mr. Brownjohn.' Coverdale was looking at him with what might have been pity. Beside him, Sergeant Amies was holding the Easonby Mellon letters. 'No more questions for to-night.'

CHAPTER THREE

LIFE GOES ON

He stayed that night, and for two nights after it, with the Elsoms. Derek—he had insisted that Arthur should call him by his Christian name—had come to The Laurels and taken him back. No sooner was he in the Elsoms' home than a doctor arrived. He turned out to have been sent by Coverdale. He took Arthur's pulse, listened to his heart, looked into his eyes, ordered him to bed immediately and gave him two pills which, with the accompanying glass of hot milk, sent him to sleep in five minutes. He woke next morning to find that Elsom was working in the garden—it was Saturday. Melissa brought him coffee and toast on a tray.

So began two of the most enjoyable days in his life. Melissa was prepared to treat him like an invalid, and he stayed in bed that Saturday until lunchtime. It occurred to him that he had not spent a whole morning in bed since he was a child. All sorts of people left messages of sympathy. 'I told them you were not well enough to see anybody yet,' Melissa chirped. The doctor returned and pronounced him much improved. When he got up he wore Elsom's dressing-gown, which was far too big

148

for him. In the afternoon Elsom brought a caseful of clothes from The Laurels.

'You're very kind,' Arthur kept repeating.

'Not a bit of it. You stay as long as you like, that's the way we want it. What are friends for if they don't rally round at a time like this?'

You're not a friend of mine, he felt inclined to say, I hardly know you and don't even like you. But the doggy managing quality of Elsom proved very helpful. 'Hate to bring it up, Arthur, old chap,' he said, 'But there'll be the question of the funeral. Would you like me to see Jukes, they say he's the best local man?' Then there was the coffin. Was it to be the finest quality oak with specially designed handles, or standard pattern? His choice of finest quality oak met with approval. The inquest was fixed for Tuesday, and Elsom had gathered that it would be more or less a formality.

'I think Coverdale's got a line he's working on, though he won't say much about it.' He held out a small paper bag. 'I got this for you.'

Arthur opened the bag. It contained a black tie. He saw that Elsom was wearing one.

'Just a formality, but you have to show respect.'

'Very thoughtful of you.' He took off the tie he was wearing and put on the black one. 'Thank you very much.'

That evening Melissa suggested that, if he felt up to it, they should ask one or two people

149

in to-morrow who wanted to express their sorrow in person. He dimly perceived that the Elsoms were using the occasion to establish themselves in the community, but what did it matter? A dozen people came in before lunch on Sunday, and the occasion turned out to be something between a cocktail party and a wake. The Paynes were there, and so was the retired naval commander. A dwarfish man from the Liberal Club told Arthur what a great loss Clare would be to the whole community, and Miss Leppard, secretary of the Art Society at Weybridge, said that Clare had a real talent for painting. Miss Leppard was a tall peering woman, and she brought her face very close to Arthur's as she said, 'I have had a visit from the police.' He moved back a little. 'They were interested in your wife's attendance at our classes. I told them that she had one of the most original approaches of anyone in the group. I'm not sure if that was really what they wanted to know.'

So they were on to the Weybridge art classes! He knew that they must be, but it was good to have this confirmation of it. Had they got on to the hotel yet? The trouble was that he felt a need to give them some direction. He wanted to go to Coverdale and tell him the name of the man he was looking for. That was obviously not possible, and he felt the pangs of the artist unable for private reasons to make public acknowledgment of his work.

'Wonderful weather.' That was Mrs. Payne. Had she not been saying a few days ago that the weather was incalculable? 'I shall never forget the chats poor dear Clare and I had about her garden. She loved growing things.' She put a hand on his arm. 'You mustn't take it too hard. George and I were *very* fond of you both. We always thought you were perfectly suited.'

The strange thing was, he reflected, that in many ways this was perfectly true.

The inquest was a formality as Elsom had suggested, and indeed it was rather too much of a formality to suit him. The doctor gave evidence that death had been caused by a bullet which entered the stomach and was responsible for an internal haemorrhage. The deceased had also been hit by two other bullets, one penetrating the ribs and the other grazing the left arm. Mr. Lillicrapp made a brief appearance to say that he had heard glass breaking, gone round to the garden, seen the body, and telephoned the police. Nothing at all was said about the man he had seen. Coverdale popped up to say that police inquiries were continuing. The coroner adjourned the inquest *sine die*, which Arthur gathered meant until they had some more evidence. The funeral was interesting in its way, although it was something of a trial because certain members of the Slattery connection reappeared, among them Uncle Ratty. He was visibly older and now walked with a stick, but age had not made him less choleric. 'Should never have left her.'

'What's that?'

'Used to write, say she was lonely.' This was a new light on Clare. Had she really been lonely? Such a possibility had never occurred to him. 'Left her at the mercy of these damned young thugs. That's who it was, take it from me. Army discipline, that's what they want.' It did not seem worth arguing the point.

After the funeral he returned to The Laurels. The Elsoms protested at his going, but not very fervently. He guessed that they had had enough of him, or to put it unkindly that there was no more publicity to be got out of him. Before he went Elsom said, 'About that little deal, it's still on.'

'What deal?' He really had forgotten.

'Lektreks.' Elsom showed his teeth. 'You said Clare had objections.'

'I can't possibly consider it just now.'

'I realise that, Arthur. When you're ready GBD will still be there.'

Back at The Laurels again his first sensation was a feeling of freedom. There were certain things about the house that he had always wanted to change and now—how extraordinary it was—he could do whatever he wished. He put Mr. Slattery up in the attic and brought down one of his mother's old pictures of the Sussex downs. To his surprise Susan was enthusiastic about the change, and revealed that she had always thought the portrait very gloomy. Her attitude towards him was one of protective flirtatiousness. 'I expect you'll like me to come in a bit more. I could cook lunch and then leave something for the evening.'

'That's very kind.' He hesitated before asking her to help him change round the furniture in the livingroom, but about this too she was approving. The bloodstained sofa cover had been sent to the cleaners.

'You'll be staying here, then?' she asked after he had been back three or four days.

'I don't know. I haven't made up my mind.'

'After all, it's your home.'

'It's a big decision, Susan.' He found it easy to call her Susan now, where before it had been difficult. 'I have to try and adjust to a new life.' He longed to ask whether she had talked to the Inspector about the man she had seen in the garden, but appreciated the need for restraint.

'I can see that. Must be lonely.'

He agreed, but in fact found that he did not miss Clare at all. He seemed to be busy from morning to night, shopping, doing little things about the house and in the garden (he chopped down a vine that darkened the living-room which Clare had always refused to remove), answering the telephone, accepting and refusing invitations from people he knew only slightly. He realised that some of these people asked him as a social obligation owed to the bereaved and that others were eager to hear the unpleasant details of the act, but still the invitations pleased him and he accepted a few of them, although he was careful of what he said and careful also not to drink more than one glass of spirits or three of wine. He was even asked to a Liberal Club social, but this was one of the invitations he declined.

At two or three of these functions he saw George Payne, and the bank manager invited him in for a chat. Payne began by asking him about the crime. Were the police any nearer to finding the murderer? Arthur said he didn't know. He hadn't spoken to Coverdale since the inquest.

Payne lighted his pipe and sat back behind his fumed oak desk. 'I tell you what, the police aren't all they used to be. I don't believe all the tales I hear, but I can tell you this, if they spent their time looking for criminals instead of giving motorists tickets for doing five miles over the speed limit, we'd all be better off.' It seemed safe to agree. 'And how are things going, Arthur? How are you keeping in yourself?'

He was used to being questioned as if he had just recovered from a serious operation, and had even come to like it. The question, in any case, was a formal approach to the production of an array of papers Clare had lodged with the bank. A solicitor could handle some of these things if Arthur wished it, but otherwise Mr. Payne would take the whole burden of them upon his shoulders. He murmured that that would be very kind, and Mr. Payne said with a brisk smile, 'That's what we're here for, to help. I wish more people understood that. Now, you might like to have a look at *these*. If you come round this side of the desk I can explain.'

He explained and Arthur listened, although without full comprehension. There were stocks and Defence Bonds and things which should have been sold but hadn't been, and other things which if he took George's advice he would hang on to. There was the pass-book in which he noted, but did not mention, that large withdrawal from Clare's private account. The private account in any case contained only a small fraction of the sum that would be coming to him. With a flash of indignation he realised that Clare had had a good deal more money than he had known. He would not be a rich man, but there was enough to provide a tidy income, which indeed she had been enjoying throughout their marriage. No wonder she had been comparatively unconcerned about his earnings.

The little chat lasted more than an hour, and ended by Arthur expressing his complete faith in his friend George. 'He's really still in a state of shock, poor little chap,' the bank manager said to his wife afterwards. 'It's a good job he's got us to look after his money. I'll tell you what he is, he's unworldly.' And as a mild parting jest he said to Arthur, 'No more investments like that car cream, you know.' Little Brownjohn looked quite startled for a moment.

During these days Arthur did not once go up to London. He knew in a way that he ought to put in an appearance at the Lektreks office, but there seemed to be no hurry. If orders had come in they could wait. That was what he told himself, but the truth was that London represented to him things that he wanted to forget. There was the suitcase in the Left Luggage office, there was the Matrimonial Assistance office which was now forbidden territory, there was Joan. He had a vision of the Matrimonial Assistance office with the letters inside the door piling up and up, until at last the postman was unable to get them through the box. Or had Coverdale got there first, were his men even now going through the files? He felt that he had to know, yet there was no possible safe way of finding out. In case he should be tempted to do so, he stayed in Fraycut.

One day he saw an interesting item in the paper:

BLACKMAIL CHARGE.
COUPLE ARRESTED

Patricia Parker, 26, a secretary, and John Termaxian, said to have posed as her husband, appeared at Bow St. yesterday on a charge of attempting to obtain money by blackmail from Mr. X, a businessman. Mr. X said that he was in a hotel room with Parker when Termaxian, whom he believed to be her husband, burst in and demanded money. Mr. X has an invalid wife, and according to him threats were made to send her photographs of him with Miss Parker.

A meeting was arranged after Mr. X had informed the police, at which £200 in notes was handed over to Termaxian, who was then arrested. Det. Sgt. Rose said Termaxian stated on arrest: 'I only did it to put the wind up him.' Termaxian and Parker committed for trial. Bail was refused.

So they had come unstuck, probably with one of the people on his list. He couldn't help feeling pleased. He worried for half an hour over their connection with Easonby Mellon, but there seemed no danger to him in their arrest. It was unlikely that they would admit to any connection with Matrimonial Assistance— why should they? No, it was a matter of blackmailers getting their just deserts.

A couple of days after reading this newspaper item he had his second conversation with Inspector Coverdale.

CHAPTER FOUR

SECOND CONVERSATION
WITH COVERDALE

He was sitting in the garden after lunch drinking hot tea with lemon when Susan announced the Inspector. Arthur said truthfully that he had been wondering what progress was being made.

'That's why I'm here. But there's something I must say first. I'm sorry if we gave you a hard time the other night.'

'A hard time?'

'That's right. I'll admit I was a bit worried about you though my sergeant, Amies, said I had no need to be. He's got a head on his shoulders, Amies. But there's no rough stuff in this force. Police are the servants of the public, is what I say.' Coverdale's face was as shiny as his suit. 'I don't mind saying we checked on your story about going up to Birmingham. I mention it in case you're talking to Mr. Gibson. Hope it doesn't cause you inconvenience. And we checked on the train times too. There was a train at twelve-thirty you could have caught.'

'Is that so? But I didn't.'

'I'm sure you didn't, you *could* have caught it is all I'm saying. I'll be frank with you, when

158

a married woman is killed my first thought is about her husband, especially if he gets the money. And when his business is a bit shaky—' He paused.

'Yes, it's true mine is. I'm thinking of selling it.'

Coverdale nodded. He had obviously talked to Elsom. 'I'm being quite frank. You didn't have an alibi, you could have been on a train which got you down to London in time to get to Fraycut. You were an obvious suspect but for one thing.'

Arthur sipped his tea and put down the glass on the bamboo table by his side. Coverdale did not seem to know quite how he should go on. As he said afterwards to Amies, he felt sorry for the little devil, he looked so trusting even if he was a bit silly. When he broke the news as tactfully as he could, by saying that Mrs. Brownjohn had been left at home a good deal and that it was not unusual for women in such a situation to look for other masculine company, the little man was incredulous.

'I can't believe it. Not Clare. Why didn't she say something to me, I'd have done something, tried to come home more.'

She wanted a bit more than you could give her, Coverdale thought, and then reproached himself for coarseness. He produced photostats of the letters they had found, and watched the bewilderment with which Brownjohn read them.

'You found these *here*?' Coverdale told him

where they had found them. Brownjohn sat shuffling the photostats, reading bits of them. 'She didn't leave me. You see what it says in this one, she wouldn't leave me.' He continued reading, rubbing his bald head. 'I suppose it's true. I never did make her happy.'

Coverdale, who had been married since he was a copper on the beat, had two teenage daughters, and liked to think that he had always been master in his own home, felt sorry for him. 'You're right about that, she wouldn't leave you. That seems to have been at the back of it. Ever heard of a man named Easonby Mellon?'

Brownjohn shook his head. 'Was that the man? I don't know the name.'

'He wasn't a friend of the family? Your wife's family?' Brownjohn said he thought not. Coverdale told him about the hotel at Weybridge. It was the only meeting they had been able to trace, but it was obvious from the letters that the lovers had met elsewhere. 'This meeting must have been some sort of crisis. She was due at her art class, but she didn't go to it, left a message saying she had another engagement.'

At Waterloo Station, Arthur thought. Aloud he said:

'What was he like? Is he like?'

'Pretty shifty customer. He ran some sort of shady matrimonial agency. But he's disappeared. And there's no doubt this was a premeditated thing. He took care to cover his tracks.' He described the gutting of the house at Clapham.

'What did he look like? Did he look like me?'

It was a bit pathetic. From what Coverdale had gathered, Mellon couldn't have been more unlike Brownjohn. 'Brown hair and little beard, loud clothes. Aggressive type, from what I can gather.'

'He was married.' At Coverdale's look of surprise Brownjohn explained. 'He mentions someone called Joan.'

'Yes, he was married.' The Inspector remembered the ludicrous story told him by Mellon's slatternly wife in the furnished bed-sitter where she was living, the tale about her husband working for some cloak and dagger organisation. She had seemed very upset by the news that he had been carrying on with another woman. It had occurred to Coverdale that the tale about being in some sort of Government service might be true, all sorts of unreliable people were employed nowadays, though he had been unable to get any confirmation of it. But the odds were heavily on Mellon being some sort of crook, and the 'Flexner' who had called on him being a fellow crook who had been looking for him. The likelihood of this was emphasised by the fact that a number of fingerprints had been found in Mellon's office which, when checked with the photomicrograph, revealed themselves as obvious forgeries, lacking the sweat pores of genuine prints. The obvious conclusion was that Mellon's prints were on file, and he had taken the wife along for a session with the Rogues' Gallery pictures, although he had known in advance that the session would be abortive. Indeed, she had told him as much, and the truth was she seemed quite besotted with the man. 'If he is there I shan't tell you,' she said, but he had been watching her, and he did not think she saw a face she recognised. The problem was to find Mellon.

'Was she upset?'

'Who? Oh, the wife. Yes, she was.' She did seem to have had a presentiment about his not coming back to her on that night when, for some unexplained reason Mellon had walked out on her and set fire to their flat. *I knew he was going for good*, she had said. *I knew my life was finished, finished*. The things people said! 'She seemed very upset.'

Brownjohn had put down his unfinished glass of lemon tea and was standing up, looking over his neat garden. 'You think he did it?'

'He was seen leaving the house at the time, sir. By your neighbour, Mr. Lillicrapp. That and the fact that he's disappeared—'

'Is there any news of him?'

'We shall find him,' Coverdale said, with a confidence he felt. 'When we really spread the net, sir, the fish don't wriggle out of it.'

Brownjohn turned to him. His voice was high. 'Thank you for telling me.'

Coverdale felt more uncomfortable than ever. 'I left it a day or two until you were feeling better. You had to know some time.'

'Quite right. You've broken it to me as gently as possible.' Hesitantly, like a schoolboy asking whether he might be allowed to leave the room, he said, 'Do you want me any more?'

'Want you?'

'This has been a shock. If I had that man here I might—I don't know. Why did he do it?'

'Looks like jealousy, sir. It's in the letters. If you'd like me to leave them—' But Brownjohn was thrusting back the photostats at him with a shaky hand.

'I don't want to read them, how could you think I should want to read them again.' He checked himself. 'I'm sorry. What I wanted to say was that I think I shall have to leave here.'

Stolidly but with sympathy the Inspector said, 'I understand.'

'It all belonged to Clare and not to me. Everything reminds me of her.' He waved a hand that embraced the garden with its rockery and the foursquare bulk of the red brick house.

Coverdale said again that he understood. He went away and left Brownjohn in the garden staring at the house in the sunlight, with the half-finished glass of lemon tea beside him on the bamboo table. He may be a silly little man, the Inspector thought, but I shouldn't like to be in Mellon's shoes if this chap ever caught up with him.

CHAPTER FIVE

A CAR AND A HOUSE

He had told Coverdale nothing but the truth. As he sat in the house every evening, eating a meal which he bought from the deep freeze at the grocer, and switching the television set on and off in the hope of finding a programme to interest him, he felt Clare's presence pervading the rooms as tangibly as a scent. He was not burdened by guilt about the act, which seemed something remote and belonging to another person, nor did he feel any sense of triumph that things had gone as he intended. It was rather as if Clare was not dead at all but might walk through the front door at any moment, criticise the changes he had made in the house and demand that everything be put back in its proper place. He had moved the television set to a part of the room where it was possible to sit and watch in comfort, but he knew that she would be annoyed because it made all the furniture look unbalanced. He hung up some curtains that Clare had discarded because she thought them too bright, but they gave him little pleasure. There were some things that he enjoyed doing himself, like paying the milkman, and there was the daily pleasure of shopping, but even about such things there was something disconcerting, because he was constantly reminded that he was shopping not for two but for one. After buying a chop one day he remembered that Clare did not like chops, and felt irritation because she would not be there to see his gesture of independence. He was irritated also by Susan's complaisance, which had pleased him so much at first. Why was she so unctuously friendly, why could she not behave more as she had done when Clare was alive? He contemplated getting rid of her, but found himself unable to make the effort.

He spent the whole of one evening up in the attic, dismantling the slot racing track with the intention of bringing it down and setting it up in the dining-room, which he hardly ever used. After all, he could do what he liked, he could even knock two rooms into one to accommodate the track if he wished. But he found that he no longer had any interest in slot racing, and never put up the track again. He advertised and sold the whole thing through a local paper.

He found himself unwilling to leave the house for any length of time. He was not afraid that something might be discovered in his absence, for there was nothing to discover, but each time he opened the front door he had a feeling that something terrible might have happened. This sensation became so strong that he was increasingly reluctant to go out in the evening. There was no lack of invitations, from the Paynes, the Elsoms and others, but he refused them with transparently untruthful excuses. Nor did he go up to London. Easonby Mellon's clothes were in the Left Luggage office still, together with the diary, and he knew that he must do something about them, but he stayed at The Laurels.

One evening Payne came round, bringing with him some papers for signature. He accepted a glass of sherry.

'Nice bright curtains. You've made some improvements.' He peered at Arthur as if he were an object at the end of a microscope. 'How are you keeping, old chap? Sorry you haven't been able to manage an evening for bridge.'

'I've been busy. And you need a couple.'

'Nonsense,' Payne said heartily, although it was obviously true. 'You're looking a bit peaky.'

'I'm all right.'

'Partly the weather, I dare say. It's a funny old summer all right,' the bank manager said judicially, although it had been very much like all the summers Arthur could remember. 'You want to get away. And you're a lucky fellow, you can do it.'

This was a day or two after Coverdale's visit, and the words seemed to harden the resolution in Arthur's mind. 'I thought of selling the house.'

'I quite understand. Though of course we shall be sorry to lose you. Where did you think of going?'

Nothing so tangible as a particular place had been in his mind, and it was with surprise that he heard his reply. 'A little place by the coast. Somewhere near Brighton.'

From the moment of speech he knew that this was what he wanted. It was as though a gate had been opened by the words, and after Payne had gone he brought down from the attic the other water colours and sat in a chair looking at them. The memories they evoked filled the room. His mother's sprawling hand had given them titles: 'Devil's Dyke in Summer,' 'West Blatchington, the Mill,' 'Penn's House and Cottage, Steyning,' and so on. The longer he looked at them the more attractive they seemed. They were very different from Clare's pictures, in which great blocks of vivid colour filled the canvas, barely recognisable as tables and chairs. What nonsense Miss Leppard had talked about Clare showing talent—his mother's water colours seemed to him ten times more interesting. When his mother painted she had worn always a large floppy hat which kept away the intense sunlight. He had asked her once whether she could see clearly enough, and she had laughed and said coquettishly, 'Even a lady painter has to look after her complexion, darling.' It was true that she had a complexion of beautiful pallor with just the faintest hint of colour in it—or had the colour, now that he came to think of it, been added by art?

They had lived at Brighton for only twelve months, after she separated from his father, but in retrospect the time seemed to have been much longer. In his recollection that had not been a funny old summer, but one in which day after day had been hot with a sky of endless blue. He did not know until years later that his father had gone off to live with the other woman whom he eventually married, only that there were no more quarrels every evening, and that he must not mention his father's name. 'You're all I have now,' his mother said to him. 'We shall never be parted, shall we, darling?' Every day they had taken a picnic somewhere on the downs and there, on a green breast of hill, she sat and dabbed paint on to cartridge paper while he read historical tales and funny stories, or rolled on the grass.

He remembered vividly being at the top of a hill, calling to her to watch and then rolling down, over and over until he came to rest at the bottom. He saw that blood was running down one of his knees and began to cry. He looked up then to the top of the hill, an immense distance, and saw her against the skyline, arms spread out like a bird's wings, and then descending to him with little musical cries of alarm. They went almost always to the downs, because his mother said that Brighton itself was vulgar. Sometimes they caught a bus and had tea at Steyning in a little low-ceilinged cottage where he always drank milk with soda water, which she said was good for him. Was it possible that this period in his life had lasted for only a few months? He had never returned to that part of Sussex, but looking at the water colours with their patches of green, gold and blue, he knew that this was where he wished to live.

Later that evening he contemplated his own naked figure in the full length bedroom mirror, the spindly legs and sloping shoulders, the beginnings of a paunch, and below the paunch the thin fuzz and the small useless-looking penis. He examined closely the egg head with its small sorrowful eyes like raisins, and the poached egg pouches beneath them. 'Not much of a body,' he said aloud, and it occurred to him that it was the same body with which Easonby Mellon had been so successful. That too seemed a long time ago, everything before the act was a long time ago.

For a few days after the act he had felt an intense urge to recommence writing his diary, and suffered the sense of deprivation that a smoker feels on giving up cigarettes. He actually bought a note-book and sat down to write in it, but the words refused to flow as they had done in the past. After a couple of days in which he found almost nothing to say, he tore out the sheets on which he had written and burned them. This gesture seemed to have a symbolic value. After it he was better able to accept that he had entered a world in which the pressures and pleasures of the past no longer existed. He did not want the things that Easonby Mellon had taken so greedily, nor was he the Arthur Brownjohn who had been married to Clare. The act had in some mysterious way set him free to begin a new life. He felt himself able to go to London.

He went to the Lektreks' office in Romany House and found there a few orders and several sharp letters from his American suppliers asking why they had not heard from him. In a burst of energy he typed twenty letters in a day, informing suppliers and customers that because of family troubles Lektreks was closing down. Then he invited Elsom to lunch and told him the news.

'But you can't do that.' Elsom was amazed and indignant.

'Why not?'

'I told you, GBD are interested. You're throwing away money.'

Although the problems of the past were

remote he recognised that they existed, and that it would be foolish to let GBD see the Lektreks books. He said curtly that the closing down of Lektreks was his affair.

'Of course it is.' Elsom spat out bits of food in his earnestness. 'But I'm speaking as a friend, Arthur, you understand. You can't do anything but lose by this.'

'It's what Clare would have wished,' he said piously, and added with more truth, 'It's for my own peace of mind.' The meal was concluded in gloomy silence.

There remained the question of Easonby Mellon's relics and the diary. They could not be left indefinitely at Waterloo Station, but he had not faced up to the problem of their disposal. When he had collected them, where were they to be buried or burned? It struck him suddenly that he must buy not only a house but a car. If he possessed a car, the disposition of Mellon's belongings would be simplicity itself.

No sooner had the idea occurred to him than the purchase of a car seemed a matter of urgency. He had learned to drive in the army during the war, but he took a few lessons and surprised his instructor by his aptitude and the quickness of his reactions. There was little point in having a car until he had passed the driving test, but he was unable to deny himself the pleasure of spending money. He did not buy a new car because part of the pleasure lay in bargaining about the price, and after visiting half a dozen dealers and trying out twice that number of cars he bought a two-year-old Triumph, guaranteed by the dealer to have had only one owner and to be in splendid condition. The car was driven back to The Laurels and put into the garage, which had been cleared to receive it. He waited eagerly for the day when he would take the test.

In the meantime he was engaged in selling The Laurels and buying a house on the Sussex downs. He slightly scandalised Jaggard, the estate agent, who hinted delicately that the recent tragedy might affect the price, by asking what would be a reasonable figure and then naming a sum two hundred and fifty pounds below it. The Laurels was bought by a civil servant who had a wife and family, and the sale was completed in August. Arthur had, however, already moved out. There was a sale of effects, a symbolic severance of the bonds that linked him to Clare. He included all of their household belongings in this sale, even things that would obviously be needed in his new home like kitchen utensils and the lawn mower. He did not attend the sale, but was pleased to see that the picture of Mr. Slattery had fetched only three pounds, the cost of the frame.

He said as few good-byes as possible. What, after all, linked him to Fraycut now that life with Clare was over? The Paynes, the Elsoms, one or two others, said how sorry they were to see him go, but he did not feel that they were in any way his friends. Perhaps it was a good thing that Arthur Brownjohn, starting a new life, should have no friends. He gave Susan a cheque for a hundred pounds, saying that Clare would have wished her to have it, and was embarrassed by a flood of tears. He had a slightly disturbing encounter when he was almost knocked down while crossing a street one day by a car which swung without warning out of a side road.

The driver poked his head out of the window and shouted at him. 'You want to bloody well look where you're going.' It was Doctor Hubble. He got out of the car and stood swaying slightly. 'Oh, it's you. How are you? Hear you're clearing out.'

Arthur agreed, although they were not the words he would have chosen.

'Don't blame you. Shouldn't want to stay myself in the circumstances.' What did he mean by that? 'Still haven't got the chap who did it?'

'No.'

Hubble stood glaring at him, and Arthur felt a twinge of uneasiness. How could he ever have tried deliberately to deceive a man who resembled more than anything else a dangerous wild animal? Then the doctor stuck out his hand, said 'She was a damned fine woman,' got back into the car and drove away.

Before he left he went to see Coverdale. The Inspector's reception of him was friendly but gloomy. There was no news of Mellon.

'We've found somebody who saw him on the platform. Carrying a blue suitcase.' A shiver went through Arthur's frame. This was the suitcase in the Left Luggage office. If the police ever thought of searching there ... but why should they do any such thing? Coverdale was still talking. ' ... up in London I guess, hiding out. A crook like Mellon knows plenty of places. But we'll find him.'

'You don't think he's gone abroad.'

'I don't. One thing, far as we can tell he's got no passport. No, he's hiding out. Trouble is, we don't know who his friends are. Can't find out how he got to know your wife either.'

Arthur shook his head to show that he also could not imagine how this had come about. Then he said with careful slowness, 'You've questioned his own wife again, I suppose?'

Coverdale stared at him. The shiny lumps on his face were more than usually apparent. 'You hadn't heard?'

'Heard what?'

'She's dead. Put her head in the gas oven.'

On the wall behind the Inspector there was a photograph of police sports, with a man doing the pole vault, twisting over the bar. Arthur stared at this photograph.

'Can't think what made her do it. Wish I had talked to her again, got to the bottom of all that rubbish about Mellon being an agent.'

'When did it happen?'

'Fortnight ago. It was in the papers. She left the usual note, can't go on, that kind of thing.'

A secretary came in with letters to be signed. Coverdale said, 'We'll keep in touch. Don't worry. The usual channels work slowly sometimes, but everything comes through them in the end.'

After leaving the station he walked to a small public garden and sat down on one of the green wooden benches surrounding a dry fountain topped by a mournful bronze bust. Below the bust it said: 'These gardens are the gift of Ezekiel Jones, citizen of this borough, educator and philanthropist.'

He knew that he should feel sorrow and remorse, but in fact he felt nothing. What had she said to him on that last evening? *Can't live without you, I shall kill myself*, something like that. People really do kill themselves, this is something that happens, he thought. He tried to remember what Joan looked like, but was unable to bring her face before his eyes. He seemed insulated from emotion, as though some fibrous barrier had been interposed between his feelings and what went on in the world.

An old man sat down on the bench, produced a bag of bread from his pocket and began to break the bread and throw bits to the pigeons clustering round him. One of the pieces fell beside Arthur's foot. He picked it up and threw it to a bird that seemed weaker than the rest. The pigeon looked at the bread, pecked at it ineffectually, then moved away. None of the other pigeons came near it.

He found a house soon after he moved into a Brighton hotel and began to look for one. He found the house quickly because he knew what he wanted. The area between Devil's Dyke and Brighton, which he remembered with pleasure, proved distressingly urbanised and unattractive. Perhaps the beauty of it had been invented by him and it had always been like this, for he learned with surprise that a railway had run to the Dyke before the war. The triangle to the east of this area, however, topped by Ditchling Beacon, with its small villages and relics of ancient earthworks, fascinated him. He knew from the map that this was not where he had come in childhood, yet it seemed to him that he recognised landmarks, the Iron Age fort of Hollingbury, Plumpton Plain, and the black and white windmills known as Jack and Jill. It was here, near to the road running from Ditchling to Brighton, that he bought a small bungalow, surprising another estate agent by his acceptance of the price asked for it. The bungalow had been built in the nineteen thirties, of ochre brick now weathered to neutral brown. It had a square living-room with french windows, two bedrooms of which one was minute, a surprisingly large kitchen with a good deal of electrical equipment in it, and a bathroom with green tiles on the wall and mustard coloured plastic tiles on the floor. Geese flew on the living-room walls. It was not pretty, but nothing could have been less like The Laurels, and the setting was delightful, sheltered in a small cleft between hills. Outside there was a garage and a quarter of an acre of wilderness which had once been a garden. He was able to move in before the end of August, and he drove the Triumph into the garage himself, for a week before the move he passed his driving test.

Almost the first thing he did was to put up his mother's water colours in the sitting-room. For some reason he did not take down the flying geese. Did he leave them because, like the water colours, they would have offended Clare? Had he bought the bungalow because it was what she would have described as a potty little place? He could not be sure, but in any case this was a line of thought that he did not care to pursue. The furniture came from a Brighton store. It was all new and mostly finished in light woods, polished pine and afromosia. On the afternoon that he moved in, there was a knock on the door. He opened it to find a diminutive couple standing there smiling at him.

'Mr. Brownjohn?' The little man took off a check cap and presented a card. 'George

Brodzky.'

'And I'm Mary,' the little woman chirped. 'We're your neighbours.'

'Neighbours?'

'Over the hill. From Dunroamin. You must have passed it. So amusing, English names, are they not?'

That was George. Mary chimed in. 'And we thought as you were moving in—I mean, we know what it's like—you would come to tea.'

'Come to tea!' The note of horror in his voice escaped them.

'Tea is on the hob.' Little George rubbed his hands.

'You're very kind but—'

'I won't take no for an answer,' said little Mary. 'I've made some buns, and although I say it myself my buns are good. And you'll find the men get on *much* better without you, isn't that right?' She called this out to the foreman, who agreed enthusiastically. Arthur had been altogether too fussy about occasional bumps and splinterings.

'Her buns are the tops,' said George.

He went to tea with the dismal knowledge that he would regret it. The Brodzkys lived over the brow of the hill, five minutes' walk away, in a bigger version of his bungalow. Brodzky was a Jewish tailor who had come over as a refugee from the Nazis, and had evidently done rather well. Sufficiently well, at least, to retire and buy the bungalow which had been named Dunroamin in what Mary told George was the English tradition. It was not about themselves that they wanted to talk, however, but about their new neighbour. They knew he was alone, but what had happened to his wife? Arthur said she had died recently, and did not expand on it. He did not need to, however, for Mary Brodzky read about every case of criminal violence in the newspaper.

'Not *the* Mr. Brownjohn?' She saw from Arthur's hesitancy that he was. 'George, Mr. Brownjohn's wife was—this was the case that—you know, you read about it—'

'The lady who was murdered?' Little George rubbed his hands together.

She lowered her voice respectfully at mention of the tabooed word. 'Such a terrible thing, and they still haven't got the man, have they?'

No doubt the manner of Clare's death would have became known quickly in any case, but he felt that acceptance of the invitation had been disastrous. When he went into the local general shop or into the nearby pub conversation ceased for a moment before being abruptly resumed, and he saw people looking at him with sidelong expectancy. Mary Brodzky twice telephoned him with invitations to meet people, both of which he refused, and one day she called to ask if she could do any shopping for him in Brighton. He replied politely that he was driving in himself. On the

179

following day George called. It was raining.

'We have here in the village our society for amateur dramatics. I am to ask if you would like to join.' His smile was wide.

'No, thank you.'

'It is very amusing. Perhaps if I should explain it—'

Brodzky was not wearing a coat. Rain spotted his shoulders. It was outrageously rude not to ask him in. 'Go away,' Arthur said.

Brodzky was dumbfounded. 'I beg your pardon?'

He was dismayed to hear his voice rising to an undignified squeak. 'I don't let nosy parkers into my house.' He stepped back and slammed the door. After that there were no further invitations from the Brodzkys, and they did not acknowledge each other in the street.

That was really the end of his relations with the village. In the shop he was greeted politely but without warmth, and he stopped going to the pub. The milkman said good day to him and the butcher delivered three times a week. The vicar called once, but lost interest when he learned that his new parishioner did not go to church. The Brodzkys had offered to try to find a woman who would come in and do for him, but their relations had been severed soon afterwards and he felt reluctant to allow anybody to intrude on his affairs, asking personal questions and poking about among his things. The bungalow was small, and it was

180

quite easy to clean it himself without the nosy assistance of some Sussex Susan. He had escaped from them all, Susans, Elsoms, Paynes and the rest. He was, as he had often wished to be, alone.

He found sufficient occupation inside and outside the house. He bought a multi-purpose electric tool with which he sanded and polished the floors of both living-room and bedrooms, repainted them, built some bookshelves and also a cupboard for the living-room. The making and fitting of this cupboard, which was made of a polished wood named sangrosa, gave him great emotional satisfaction, and he put a small compartment inside it, with its own separate doors. The latch on these inner doors did not fit perfectly and had a tendency to come open, but still he was delighted by his own skill. The garden also took up a good deal of time. What could be done with a quarter of an acre? He bought half a dozen books on gardening and cut out articles that appeared in the papers. He would have liked to see things flowering immediately, but it proved that September was not a good time for planting. However, there were things that could be done. He reduced the wilderness of the lawn with a scythe, mowed it, and then spiked the mossy weedy surface with an aerator. Every day for a week he carried out destructive operations, pulling up weeds and nettles and burning them in a new kind of incinerator which he bought. Sodium chlorate extinguished weeds on the paths. There was broken fencing at the back of the house which he mended with new palings and wire. He worked every morning and afternoon, eating a quick lunch of bread and cheese with an urgency he could not have explained even to himself. In the evening he cooked something, often out of a tin, and settled down to read the papers and watch television. The news seemed unreal to him, the capers on the screen even more insignificant, and watching them he often fell asleep.

One day he took the train to London, went across to Waterloo Station, collected the blue suitcase and came straight back again. In spite of his advance trepidation he felt no flicker of fear when he handed over the ticket and was given the suitcase. He would have been quite prepared to meet Coverdale at the station. Easonby Mellon had had a blue suitcase, he was carrying one too. What was strange about that? He was strong in the assurance of success. He would not have been so boastful as to call what he had done perfect, for he recognised that he had been helped by one or two fortuitous circumstances like Mr. Lillicrapp's sight of Easonby Mellon leaving The Laurels, but still he was satisfied.

He deliberately delayed opening the suitcase until the evening, leaving it to be savoured like a favourite sweet. As a further congratulatory gesture, a measure of Brownjohn's confidence in Brownjohn, he opened the sangrosan cupboard, considered the bottles which had been lined up there— gin, whisky, vodka—and opened the whisky. Gobble gobble, went the liquid in the glass, giving him a delicious feeling, not unlike that felt by Easonby Mellon when having a bit of nonsense. A zizz of soda and there it was, ready for drinking. He drank. Then he took the little key from his ring and turned it in the lock of the suitcase. Was everything there? He checked, hugging himself.

Item. One suit in loud gingery tweed, jacket and trousers only, in good condition.

Item. Tie decorated with small coloured horseshoes, sporty shirt and ditto socks.

Item. One fine head of glossy red-brown hair, one small beard of slightly different colour. One small bottle of spirit gum.

Item. One pair of contact lenses in small box.

Item. One diary in black cover.The rest of Easonby Mellon's clothes, together with two of his wigs, had been incinerated at Clapham. He stroked the crisp hair.

'Safely home,' he said aloud. 'Safely home, my beauties.' He drained the whisky and poured another, then opened the diary and sat down to read, absorbed by the account of problems that had loomed so large in the past and now looked trivial. All the fear he had

183

expressed about Hubble, for instance, and his feeling that the doctor had been suspicious. Obviously what he had taken for suspicion was natural drunken rudeness, the 'terrible glare' he had noted was annoyance at being called so late at night. At the same time he was pleased that he had given up the zincalium scheme, which as he saw now had been clumsily conceived. When he came to the passages about Clapham the past flooded back unpleasantly. To stop himself from reading further he took out the sheets, tore them up into small pieces, and put them into a cardboard box. To-morrow would be D-Day, D for Destruction. His glass was empty, and he poured another drink. He took off his jacket and trousers, put on the tweed suit, clapped the wig to his head without bothering to use the fixative. Easonby Mellon walked again!

Not quite, however, not really as he should be. He used the spirit gum to fix the beard and put in the contact lenses, which were more trouble than they should have been because his hand was shaking slightly. 'Not a bad little bachelor establishment you've got here, Brownjohn,' he said. 'You don't mind if I look around?' He strutted into kitchen and bedroom commenting loudly on them, bouncing up and down on the bed. He went to the front door, opened it with a little difficulty and staggered slightly as he walked out to the garden, looked up at the green swell of hill.

'Nestling under the down,' he said. 'Very nice, though it's nicer to nestle between the sheets.' It was twilight, and the air was filled with the sweet scent of early evening. He sniffed this air, opened his mouth and drank up the air in great gulps, staring at the green hill. A tickling sensation at the back of his neck made him turn.

The Brodzkys stood beside the gate, arm in arm, staring at him. The little man with his check cap, the little woman gazing eager-eyed—for a few seconds they stared at him and he stared back at them. Then the Brodzkys, still with arms linked like some four-legged creature, scuttled away up the road to their bungalow, and he returned to the house. He stared at himself in the bedroom glass. He seemed to have shrunk within the clothes, which hung on him with curious looseness—could he have lost weight? With furtive speed he took them off, together with the wig and moustache, and slipped out the contact lenses. Safely back in Arthur Brownjohn's nondescript old flannel trousers he recorked the whisky bottle and returned it to the cupboard. The latch came open and he closed it with a thump. The genie who had come out of the bottle lacked his old magical power.

On the following morning he put a barrowful of weeds into the incinerator, stuffed the suit on top of them together with the box containing the torn-up diary, and added the beard. He broke up the contact lenses with a hammer and added them to the pile, and did the same thing with the bottle of spirit gum. Then he put on more weeds and set fire to the lot. Blue smoke swirled upwards. He placed the top on the incinerator and left the past to burn. At the last moment he found himself unable to dispose of the wig. As he stroked the crisp reality of the hair tears came to his eyes. He put it carefully into the inner compartment of the cupboard, promising himself that he would destroy it very soon. At midday he lifted the incinerator lid and stared at the contents that were reduced to satisfying but saddening ash.

Although so much of the past had gone his mother's water colour scenes remained. He took down the little pictures from the walls, put them into the car, and drove out over the downs. During the afternoon he revisited the scene of each picture, and found them all changed. 'West Blatchington, the Mill' had been shown as an idyllic rural scene, but it stood now among a spate of suburban building. 'The Downs at Peacehaven' bore no resemblance to the hills dotted with a pretty house or two shown in her mild greens and blues. Instead, a great mess of brick sprawled over the whole area like some terrible red growth. Not one of the scenes was as she had shown it. He knew that this was to be expected, yet it troubled him. The country to-day belonged to the new housing complexes and the petrol pump. The world of his childhood, the world his mother painted, had been destroyed. Back in the bungalow he pored over the water colours as though they could provide an answer to the problems of his life, and realised what was wrong. According to a book he had read about Sussex the picture of the Devil's Dyke should have shown a railway where she depicted a green wash of down. She had left out the railway because it would have spoiled the picture. Were the other paintings equally remote from reality? When he looked up other books he found that Peacehaven in the early nineteen twenties could not possibly have looked as she had shown it, and it seemed to him that this doubt about the veracity of the pictures must extend to the whole of his childhood life. Had it ever really existed as he remembered it? His mother had died of what was then called heart disease when he was twenty-one. How much did he really know about her? Did this image of a woman in a floppy hat, this indulgent mother trying to preserve him from the harshness of the world, correspond with the truth? How deep had been her disappointment when it became clear that he was not bright enough to get a University scholarship and would have to take a job when he left grammar school? What had she felt during the last years in the little flat at Swiss Cottage where she died? It was not until the funeral that he had seen his father again, and then he wondered how he had ever felt the fear he was now able to acknowledge of this outspoken but meticulously neat and dapper man. They found little to say to each other, but they met two or three times a year, conversing with the politeness of strangers. His father had written a letter of sympathy after Clare's death which remained unanswered.

These events were clouded in his mind, he had always refused to discuss them with himself, and it seemed to him that the rest of his life must consist of such an unending discussion. He could remember nothing at all of the years before his mother's death when he had left school and gone to work at the insurance office in which he had stayed until his call-up. Had he come home each evening to a cooked meal, did they ever go out together? He could remember nothing except the three heart attacks she had suffered in the months before she died, the rest was the woman in the floppy hat on the downs painting her untrue pictures. He had shown the pictures to Clare just after their marriage, and a little later she had begun to attend art classes. Was it possible that his feelings about his mother had affected his relationship with Clare?

He hung up the pictures again, ate a tin of food and went to bed. He lay sleepless until four in the morning. Around him in the darkness stretched the barren land of freedom.

CHAPTER SIX

THE TRUE IDENTITY OF ARTHUR BROWNJOHN

He saw the Identikit picture in the paper the next morning. Under the heading HAVE YOU SEEN THIS MAN? was a composite picture of a man with thick hair, a squashy nose, large staring eyes, a little beard and the caption: 'This is an Identikit picture made with the help of eye witnesses of a man the police would like to interview in connection with the Fraycut murder case. Further details: brown hair and beard, about 5 ft. 9 inches tall, stockily built, possibly wearing tweed suit or sports jacket.' He looked at the picture and hugged himself because of its unlikeness to the facts. Two inches had been added to his height, and 'stockily built' was a tribute to the effect of the suit. At the same time he felt a little indignant about that squashy nose. His nose certainly could not be called squashy.

The Identikit picture had appeared before, although he had missed it, in the paper. It was the joint product of the recollections of the Romany House porter, the barmaid at Fraycut (who had insisted on the staring eyes), the clerk at the Weybridge hotel and Mr. Lillicrapp, as interpreted by the artist who had drawn it for the police. Inspector Coverdale had no great faith in the accuracy of the Identikit, and as usual the people who had seen Mellon were by no means agreed about such vital matters as his height, which had been placed between five feet six and five feet eleven inches. Indeed, Coverdale had no longer much expectation that they would find Mellon at all. He believed the man to be an experienced crook known to Scotland Yard under another name, that the murder had been prompted by Mrs. Brownjohn's discovery of his real identity, and that Mellon had almost certainly left the country. The best chance of laying hands on him would come when he started up another Lonely Hearts agency elsewhere, as he almost certainly would do, and Interpol had been duly alerted. In the meantime it was necessary to go through the motions.

The issue of the paper containing the Identikit picture recorded also the verdicts in the case of John Termaxian and Patricia Parker, who had received sentences of four years and nine months respectively. Termaxian had been in prison twice before for similar offences, and the Judge had referred to him as 'a blight on society, feeding on the weakness of foolish and lecherous men.' He had regarded

Parker as Termaxian's agent, and very much under his influence. There was no mention of the source from which they had obtained the name of Mr. X.

Strangely enough this paragraph depressed rather than pleased him. After reading it he went out into the garden, but worked there for only half an hour. He was in the act of turning over earth in a patch destined to be a flower border next year when an almost physical revulsion from what he was doing made him stop. He cleaned the fork and trowel he had been using, put them back in the garage, and returned to the bungalow. In the kitchen he drew himself a glass of water, sat down at a table and stared at the refrigerator. It had occurred to him that, in any meaningful sense, he did not exist. He remembered a strange novel he had read, about a man whose whole inner life had been destroyed by the things that happened to him, but who functioned perfectly to all outward appearance and even flourished, so that when he was offered an academic post 'the Faculty had no idea that it was a glacial shell of a man who had come among them' instead of a real human being. Was this his own situation? Arthur Brownjohn had wished to be free of Clare's domination, Easonby Mellon had been trapped in a net from which it had seemed essential to break out. He had escaped from Clare, he had broken out of the net, he was free—but he was forced to the conclusion that freedom only existed in relation to restriction. 'The habits by which we *live* and *think* are not what we *believe*'—that, or something like it, was what he had written in his diary. But what did he believe, what did he wish to do with his freedom? The things in which he had taken pleasure, the slot racing layout in the attic, the piles of letters round his ankles, even the bits of nonsense with Joan, seemed to have had no existence independent of the people with whom they were associated. 'I could have had the biggest slot racing layout in the country,' he thought, and had a vision of the kind of house he might have bought, a Victorian barracks with a great glass-roofed room like a monster conservatory in which the whole floor was covered with a network of tracks, bridges, fly-overs, along which there raced twenty different types of car. He could have bought such a house, he could still buy it, but he knew that he would never do so, for although he was able to conjure up the vision it no longer excited him. Slot racing had not been a passion but a reaction, a means of asserting his identity against Clare. Now that she was gone he no longer needed it. What was the true identity of Arthur Brownjohn? Surely he must take pleasure in sights and sounds, must enjoy food and want sex as Easonby Mellon had wanted it? He remembered Joan's desperate clutching at his parts in the cinema, and shuddered away from the thought that he was no more than 'a glacial shell' able to dig gardens and make cupboards but totally without emotion because heart and guts had been removed. There must be people and situations who would revive the sleeping soldier, and reveal his real nature. It was to discover them that he went to Brighton.

He watched himself with detachment, in the spirit of a doctor trying out various forms of treatment. The drive through the downs and along the main road, now, did that excite him? The sense of achievement he felt in first handling a car had long since vanished, but now he deliberately accelerated to pass other cars on bends and at the brows of hills, answering blares of protest with furious hooting of his own. At one point he passed another car near the top of a hill to find a great Bentley coming at him. He cut in sharply on the car he had just passed, which was forced to brake suddenly. Both the Bentley and the car behind him hooted, and this time he did not trouble to hoot back. 'Any emotion involved there, Mr. Brownjohn, exhilaration, fear, anything at all?' the doctor asked, and he had to shake his head in reply. He had felt nothing. Yet that was not quite true, for he had taken avoiding action, so that the instinct of self-preservation must still exist. In the pleasure of realising this he passed and cut in on another car. In the town he parked the car just behind the Palace Pier.

Come to Doctor Brighton who cures all ills. Is the prognosis favourable, Doctor? Too soon to tell, my son. For an hour he bathed in the fantasy of the Royal Pavilion. Below the onion domes he wandered in a Chinese and Indian dream, columns sprawling out as palm trees, tented ceilings down which crawled gilded dragons, great wall paintings of Chinese landscapes like those that made the Music Room resemble a lacquer cabinet. Would it be possible to live in such a cabinet, in such a world? Pagodas and temples, formal rippling rivers with sampans frozen on them as though in the performance of a ritual, palm trees and bamboos, furnishings that dazzled the senses by their colour and disturbed them by their ornamentation—he found himself thinking first that these existed in a different world from that of his mother's water colours and then that the furniture would never have done for Clare and The Laurels. He laughed aloud at the thought, and an attendant gave him a reproving glance.

After the Pavilion the Lanes, those narrow alleys right in the heart of the town, bounded by North, West and East Streets, and stuffed with antique shops where in the summer American voices could be heard translating everything into the music of dollars. He drifted from shop to shop, staring at collections of Victorian fire irons, at panelled pine mantelpieces, at windows full of old medals.

One shop window had a crowd around it, and mixing with them he saw that it held a collection of chamber pots of different sizes. He was about to turn away when he noticed a number of soapstone figures on a shelf above. One of them was his Buddha! He pushed his way through the crowd and entered the shop. A woman in a green dress greeted him. He pointed to the figure.

'The Buddha?' She took it off the shelf, her red-tipped fingers caressed it. 'You like him? I think he's fun.' She told him the price on the base. It was half what he had paid in London.

'I wanted to know—I wonder if you could tell me where you bought it?'

'I'm not sure that I know, and even if I did know it isn't policy to say.'

'I have a special reason. I believe it is—that is, it once belonged to me.'

She nodded in a humouring way and went to the back of the shop. When she came back she said, 'I bought it at a country sale. Nearly a year ago. Shouldn't admit I've had it for a year, should I, but you see I'm frank.'

A year ago! He said something confused about that being impossible. She raised her thin, plucked eyebrows. 'They're not very uncommon, you know.'

'Not very uncommon?' The man had told him it was a piece of individual Indian craftsmanship.

'I'm a terrible saleswoman, but yes, that's

right. Quite a lot of them were made in several sizes. I'd consider an offer. Since we've had it so long.' Her lips curled. They were thin, but a Cupid's bow had been painted over them.

'No, thank you. I'm afraid it's a mistake, I thought it was the one I had.'

'Perfectly all right. Don't you think it's a fun window?'

'Window?' He stared in alarm at the clear glass.

'*You* know. The indispensable article of bedroom furniture. Draws the crowds, but nobody comes in to buy.' She smiled now with an open mouth. He saw her teeth, white and regular, and the dark cavern behind them.

'No, thank you,' he said meaninglessly, and edged his way out. It did not matter, nothing at all was affected by it, but he was upset by a feeling that he had been tricked again.

What did he expect Brighton to do for him? He hardly knew. He walked uncertainly along to the Marine Parade, along the promenade towards the West Pier, and then on to the beach. He began to throw stones into the sea. The stones were smooth and cool in his palm, and as he flung them, with a jerky round arm motion, some memory stirred in his mind which he was unable to trace. There were few people on the beach, but a boy came and stood beside them and then began to pick up and throw stones himself. The boy made them skim over the water, bouncing several times before they disappeared.

'That was a sevener,' he said after one particularly good throw. Arthur flung a stone which sank ignominiously without bouncing at all. 'You don't do it right.'

'I expect not.'

'You want to get flat stones. Then like this.' He sent one skimming like a speedboat. 'See?'

The memory came back to him. On one of the rare days when they stayed in Brighton his mother had left him playing on the beach. He had joined half a dozen other boys around a boat, and they had laughed at him first because he would not go into the sea (his mother had told him it was too rough) and then because he could not throw stones properly. 'You throw like a girl,' they said. He had been weeping when his mother returned.

'You got the time, mister?'

'Ten minutes past six.'

'I got to get back to tea.'

'Wait a minute, I'll walk with you.'

The boy looked at him with the fearfulness shown by the young at any kind of involvement with their elders, then backed away. 'Wait,' Arthur appealed. He put his hand in his pocket, took out a coin, threw it. Silver glinted in the air. The boy snapped up the coin like a lizard stretching its tongue for a fly, then ran. Arthur climbed wearily up the bench, the stones hard under his feet.

Later he went on to the Palace Pier and

rode on the little electric cars. All the other cars seemed to be occupied by couples, the boys driving, the girls beside them shrieking with laughter. He steered his own car deliberately at others. After the crashes the girls laughed louder than ever. One pretty doll-like girl wore a paper hat in red, white and blue, and a badge pinned over one breast which read I AM A VIRGIN. Beneath these capitals was a small longer word—what was it? He peered to see, without success. When the ride ended and he walked off the shiny floor the couple came up to him.

'What's up, Jack?' the boy said. He was a head taller than Arthur, and he wore long sideboards.

'I beg your pardon.' He could see the word now. It was *Islander*.

'You do, eh? I said, what's up?'

'I don't know what you mean.'

'You don't? You wouldn't. He's a creep, Marilyn, I told you.'

'He's creepy,' the girl agreed, and burst into fresh peals of laughter.

He walked away down the boards of the pier. Unintelligible threats and obscenities followed him.

Seven-fifteen. He was sitting in a bar in a road parallel with the sea front sipping gin and tonic. Brighton had solved nothing, the doctor had failed. It was time to drive away again. The barman said, 'You want to see some action?' He slipped a card across the bar's shiny leatherette surface.

He nodded without knowing what was meant.

'Members only, but this'll get you in. Say Carlo sent you.'

He nodded again. The card said simply *Robin Hood*, with an address in Kemp Town. The place, when he found it, looked like a restaurant, but the door was closed. On the right hand side of it a painted and tipped arrow pointed to a bell, and he pushed this. A slit in the door opened, an eye looked at him.

'Carlo sent me.' The door opened. He confronted a girl dressed in a short jerkin and tights of Lincoln green. A green forage cap with a feather in it was set on her head, and a quiver containing arrows was slung over her shoulder.

The door closed again. The light was dim. What looked like real trees were growing on either side of him. Straight ahead he saw an oak door with the legend above it: 'Robin Hood's Cave.' To the left stood a realistic gibbet with a noose hanging from it. A voice shrieked in his ear: 'Eat ye and drink ye, my merry men.'

'What was that?'

'Jock.' The girl indicated a parrot which glared from foliage. He touched one of the trees. It was made of plastic.

'I didn't know they had parrots in Sherwood

Forest.'

'Don't touch him, he'll have your finger.' Without taking breath she went on: 'A guinea, please.'

'Carlo said this would get me in.'

'So you're in. You still pay a guinea if you want the action.'

'What action?'

She stared. The oak door opened and he saw beyond it bright light, glimpsed a roulette wheel, heard the murmur of voices. A fat man with a cigar in his mouth passed, took the coat the girl offered, and went out without speaking. 'Make up your mind,' the girl said. He paid his guinea and went towards the oak door. A figure stepped from beside the gibbet and said, 'Not carrying anything?'

'What do you mean?'

He was a large man with a broken nose, wearing jerkin and tights that seemed too small for him. His face, pitted with scars and with the eyes tiny in their folds of flesh, peered.

'That's all right, sir, you're okay.' His voice came out like water through a choked pipe.

'Why do you stand by that thing?'

'I'm supposed to be the hangman, see? They had me dressed up right, in a black mask and all, but it was too hot.' He gestured towards doors which said: 'Ye Olde Taverne of Sherwood' and 'Ye Banqueting Hall,' but Arthur went into Robin Hood's Cave.

It was a large room with panels let into the wall, depicting scenes among which he noticed Robin Hood embracing Maid Marian, giving money to the poor, defying the Sheriff, and with hands tied behind his back staring up at a gallows. Trophies of the hunt were hung about, including rather surprisingly a bear and a tiger. The brightness he had seen from outside was deceptive. Most of the room was dim. Concealed lights illuminated the wall panels and pools of light flooded down upon the tables where people were playing roulette and several card games, among which he recognised baccarat and vingt-et-un. The faces round the roulette table were reverent. They were not particularly rich faces, nor of any special class. Few were very young or very old. They were middle-aged middle-class humanity.

A hand touched his arm, a voice murmured 'This way, sir.' A young man in Lincoln green led him to a corner of the room. 'Just to get it straight, minimum stake half a crown, maximum fifty quid, fair enough?'

'I suppose so.'

'What d'you want chips for?'

A Lincoln green girl behind a counter smiled at him invitingly. Different coloured counters were arranged in front of her. He had just over twenty pounds on him. 'Five pounds' worth, please.'

The young man raised his eyebrows, said

something inaudible to the girl and drifted away. He took his counters to the roulette table and put a pound on black, ten shillings on the first twelve numbers. The number that came up was red, nineteen. This was another aspect of Doctor Brighton's treatment. Did he feel any emotion when the black and green counters were swept away, would he feel anything if he won? He could only find out by playing. In less than ten minutes he had lost his five pounds and had cashed five more. He decided to stop playing when he had lost fifteen.

His luck turned when he had three pounds left of the allotted fifteen. Numbers in the first twelve, which pays two to one, came up six times running, and when he changed to groups of four numbers, paying nine to one, he had three successive wins. He was now fifteen pounds up, and put a couple of black counters, worth a pound each, on numbers eleven and thirty-three. Number eleven turned up, a win of thirty-four pounds. He had set himself no winning limit, but it seemed a good time to stop. As his counters were translated into five-pound notes he examined his feelings, and discovered in himself no more than a mild pleasure at having beaten the table.

In Ye Olde Taverne of Sherwood, where crisps, olives and lumps of cheddar cheese came free, he ordered a large whisky. A voice behind him said, 'I saw you, you lucky man.'

The lady of the antique shop was smiling at him. She was dressed now in a black and white op art dress, the effect of which was spoiled by a conventional thick cluster of what must surely be artificial pearls. She readily accepted his offer of a drink.

'A little drinky would be very nice. It's not *my* lucky night.'

What could one say to that? He considered several conversational returns and rejected them all. They sat down at a table which had on it an ashtray shaped as a boar's head, with a hole in the mouth for the ash. She smoked a cigarette through a long holder. 'Are you a real true gambler? I *am* you know, or I would be if I had what my sainted aunt used to call the wherewithal. This is a fun place, don't you think?'

'I suppose so. It's just a gambling club, really, isn't it?'

'But don't you think the décor's brilliant? A friend of mine did it as a matter of fact, Seamus Macpherson. Of course he's really an artist, he did it to oblige Robin.'

'Robin?'

She pointed to a swarthy man wearing a dinner jacket and called, 'Yoo hoo.' The swarthy man came over. 'Robin Hood,' she said. 'Meet a new member, I don't know his name.'

'Arthur Brownjohn.'

'Welcome to Sherwood Forest. Enjoying

yourself, Mr. Brownjohn?' Robin Hood had a pencil line moustache, and looked like a Hollywood romantic actor of the nineteen thirties. His foreign accent was strong.

'He's been winning, Robin darling, of course he's enjoying himself.'

'Splendid. I hope you haven't taken us to the cleaner's.'

'What? Oh no, I only won a few pounds. I'm not a gambler.'

A bottle of champagne appeared in an ice bucket. 'To the victors the spoils,' Robin Hood said. 'That is a quotation. Don't be worried, Mr. Brownjohn, this is on the house.' Glasses were filled. 'Have you finished for the evening, or are you playing again?'

'I'm retiring while I'm a winner.' He laughed inanely, and they laughed with him.

'A wise man. But come back and see us again. Just one question.' His mouth approached Arthur's ear. 'You like the way we've fitted it out?'

'Most original.'

'A friend of Hester's. A genius. You'll forgive me.' He seized Hester's red-tipped hand, kissed it, uncoiled from his chair, and moved across the room.

'Isn't he darling? And I'll tell you something, everything he does turns to money.' She contemplated the kissed fingers as if in the hope that a Midas touch might convert them to gold. 'Of course he's not really

Robin Hood. His name's Constantin Dimitrop-something-or-other. You know those Dimitrop names. But would you believe it, I knew him when he was a waiter in a little Greek café. I don't know, do you?' He shook his head. More champagne was poured. 'D'you live around here, Arthur?'

'Just a few miles.'

'You often get in, then?'

'Sometimes.' The bottle was empty. He waved a hand, another bottle appeared, the cork popped.

'You're a bit of a dark horse,' Hester said as she drank her first glass from the new bottle. Her lips left a red smear on it. 'When you came in the shop I said to myself, "Well, you may sell him something, but be careful not to scare him off, he's the sort who scares easily." Now here you are, cool as a duke, going home with a nice little profit. How wrong can you be?'

He felt an impulse to confide. 'I do get scared, as much as anybody. But I do things, even though they scare me.'

'That's psychology. I'll tell you something. I've had that bloody shop for a year, and I've found something out. It just isn't me.'

'I thought not,' he said vaguely, although he had not thought about it.

'Oh, you're clever. You're a real dark horse.' She stubbed out her second cigarette, put away the holder, leaned over the table towards him.

205

'What would you say I *was*, really?'

The black and white of the dress dazzled him. Above it, above the diagonals that fled to infinity, was the choker. Stretch a hand, pull and the little white blobs would fly all over the room. A prize for the first man to pop an artificial pearl into the boar's head. And above the pearl choker the neck, full and unwrinkled, above the neck smooth cheeks, an inquiring nose, the red mouth a cavern. None of it excited him, he felt no stir of lust. 'An actress.'

She leaned back. 'Oh, you're so *right*. You really are a dark horse. Lavinia Skelton.'

'What?'

'My stage name. Do you like it?'

'Not very much.'

'Exactly what I said. I told that bloody agent, I told him, "Lavinia, that's Victorian, and Skelton, do you know what people will think, they'll think of a skeleton." But he was supposed to know, he said it was contemporary. Then he thought he'd done marvels when he fixed me up in a crumby little rep.' Her face approached his. 'Darling, you're cute. Why don't we have another little drinky round in my flat?'

The temptation was too great. He bent forward so that their faces were near to each other. His hand moved, pulled, the choker came away. The string broke and the pearls rolled about, just as he had foreseen, most of them on the floor but a dozen meandering

206

across the table. He picked one of them up and put it into the boar's mouth. 'Pearls in the mouth of swine,' he cried. 'First prize to me.' Laughing helplessly, he raised his champagne glass.

She clutched her neck. 'My God,' she cried. 'You bloody little barbarian.'

Things happened quickly. It seemed that everybody in the preposterous room converged on him, and that they were all angry. Without fully understanding what was happening, or why, he felt himself jerked to his feet. The glass dropped from his grasp to the floor and crunched under a foot. A hand was clasped inside his shirt collar so that he almost choked, another hand dived into his breast pocket and found his wallet. He tried to protest that they were stealing his money. Robin Hood's face appeared before him in close up, the lips bent back to reveal pale gums. 'The champagne,' he heard. 'You pay for the champagne.' Helpless, he saw a five pound note extracted from the wallet, which was then pushed back into his jacket. The grip on his shirt did not relax. Twisting to see his captor, he found that it was the man with the broken nose who had been standing beside the gibbet. In turning he tightened the grip on his neck and gasped for air.

Hester was weeping. 'My pearls. Make him pay for my pearls.'

Robin Hood's hand patted her shoulder.

'I'll buy you some more, honey. Don't worry about him, he's not worth worrying about.'

He felt himself being marched, almost carried, out of the bar. The girl who had let him in surveyed him critically. 'He got an 'at?' Broken Nose asked, and when she said no, his grip relaxed. 'Don't let 'im in again. Trouble maker.'

'You wouldn't think it to look at him. What did he do?'

''Aving a go at Hester. Trying to tear her dress off. Listen.' He pushed a big fist under Arthur's nose. 'Get out and don't come back.' The door was open. A push sent him reeling into the street. It was empty except for a man walking along the other side, whistling.

For a few moments he could do nothing except gasp. When he had got his breath he felt his neck in a gingerly way and straightened his collar. The whistling man crossed the street and walked towards him. He took out his wallet and examined the contents. They were intact except for the five pound note, which he supposed was fair enough. He became aware that something had happened, and then realised what it was. The whistling had stopped.

The man had reached the entrance of the club but had apparently changed his mind about going in. His face was half-turned away. There was something familiar about him. 'Just a minute,' Arthur said. The man quickened his step. Arthur caught up with him, put a hand on his arm, swung him round. He was looking at the sandy hair and greasy beard, the exophthalmic eyes, the twitching features, of Clennery Tubbs.

CHAPTER SEVEN

END OF A JOURNEY

He was so surprised that he let go of Tubbs's arm, but as the other accelerated, moving away from him in a walk that never quite became a trot, Arthur felt indignation move in him. But for the crookedness of this man none of his troubles would have occurred, or at least this was what he felt. 'Here,' he cried. 'Come here.'

He put a hand on Tubbs's jacket, getting a grip which was a parody of Broken Nose's hold on his shirt. The jacket began to slip away from Tubbs's shoulders, and it seemed that he might leave it. Then he stopped, turned, and said, 'What the hell d'you think you're doing?' The look of outrage was succeeded by one of astonishment which merged unconvincingly into pleasure. 'Mr. Brownjohn,' he said, as though the name were the answer to a prayer. His gaze looked beyond Arthur who half-turned with him to see that the door of the club was open and that Hester stood there.

209

She stared at them both for a moment and then retreated. The door closed again.

'I've been looking for you,' Arthur said, which was hardly the truth.

'Thought you were one of the Granger Boys. Nasty lot, have to be damn' careful down here. That place.' Tubbs jerked a thumb towards the Robin Hood. 'Some hard types in there, I can tell you.'

'You were going in.'

'Not me. I wouldn't trust myself there, not in a million years.'

'I've just come out. I won fifty pounds.'

'You did? There you are.' He spoke triumphantly, as if Arthur had proved the truth of his words. 'You can buy me a drink.'

The suggestion incensed him so much that if he had been a violent man he would have struck the other. 'You cheated me.' Unable to compass the enormity of Tubbs's offences he took refuge in a single phrase. 'You used an accommodation address.'

'I've been on the move.' Tubbs leaned against the wall under a street lamp. 'Haven't been well.'

'Rubbish.' Beneath the cloth he felt the thin bone of the arm. 'You're a scoundrel.'

'Mean it. My heart. Give me a minute.' His colour looked bad, but perhaps this was the street lighting. 'Buy you a drink.'

He continued to pull Tubbs along. He had little confidence in his power to pin the man down. Tubbs would go to the pub lavatory and never come back, or he would see some barfly acquaintance and slip away with him. 'Come home,' he said suddenly. 'I'll give you a drink there.'

'Home? Live in Brighton now, do you?'

'Just outside it. I've got my car here.'

Tubbs gave him a quick glance. 'All right then. Call at the bus station. I've left my case.'

They walked to the bus station in silence. Arthur went in and stood near while Tubbs handed over a ticket and came back with a battered fibre suitcase. 'Not sure where I'd stay,' he muttered. 'Been on the road.' When they reached the car he got in without a word.

For five minutes Arthur drove in silence. Then Tubbs spoke. 'Sorry I dropped out of circulation but I can explain, you know. Explain the whole thing.' He paused. His voice was thick, throaty. 'Something else I must say. Sympathies.'

'What's that?'

'Read about it. Very sorry.' He had linked Clare's death up with the man he swindled. 'Got the bastard who did it, have they?'

'Not yet.'

'Very very sorry, old man.' His hand snaked out and gave Arthur's a pat. 'They've got no line on this chap yet then?'

'I don't want to talk about it.' He was already regretting the impulse that had induced him to take Tubbs home. What was

211

the point of it? The man was on his uppers and there was not a chance in a thousand that he would recover any of the money. Why had he exposed himself to this wretched little crook? What did it matter? His spirits sank steadily on the way back while those of Tubbs appeared to rise. When they got out of the car he looked round inquisitively. 'Marvellous. You know you're in the country all right. Lead the way, squire.'

Would it be a good thing to drive him to the nearest station and give him his fare to London? Instead he opened the front door. Tubbs dropped his old suitcase in the hall, went into the sitting-room, sat down and looked round again.

'Very nice, very cosy. Been here long, have you?'

'Not long.'

'Moved after the tragedy from—where was it?—Fraycut, yes. You could have knocked me down with a feather when I read about it, saw your picture in the paper. I know that face, I told myself, then it clicked. It's Brownjohn, my partner. Thought of writing, never got round to it somehow.' He glanced continually at his host and away, his eyes clicking like a camera shutter. There could be no doubt that he was in a bad way. There were grease spots on his trousers, his jacket cuffs were slightly frayed, his shoes dirty. 'So you came down here. On your tod, are you?'

'I live alone, yes.'

'Live alone and like it, eh? I'm on my own too, told you that, but don't know that I should want to stay here, I have to keep moving.'

'You owe me an explanation.' He felt the absurdity of the words as he said them.

'Too right. And you owe me a drink.' He amended this hastily. 'Promised me one.'

While he opened the sangrosan cupboard and poured two whiskies the nervous yet predatory gaze of the pop eyes followed him. Tubbs talked in jerks with pauses between them. 'Had a run of bad luck since I saw you last. Left London in a hurry, put some money in a business, went phut. Went up to Manchester, lost three hundred quid in a poker game. Played against Steady Jack Malory, know him? Course, you wouldn't. Cheers.' He drank greedily.

'You swindled me.' It was difficult to feel anger. 'Wypitklere was no good.'

'No good? Oh, come on now, old man.' He hardly even pretended surprise. 'If there are any kinks in it we can straighten them out. What about putting me up for the night?'

'Certainly not.' He could not feel anger even at this suggestion.

'Really get down to details then. Still, if you won't, you won't.'

'What would be the point? I shan't see my money again, shall I? I'll write it off to experience.'

'I'll be off then.' He got up, walked over to the window, turned. 'Fact is, I'm in a temporary difficulty. Couldn't arrange a small loan, I suppose, a fiver say? Had a win this evening, you said so yourself.' *A temporary difficulty*. It was really too much. He began to laugh, then took a five pound note from his wallet, put it on the table.

'Thanks. You'll get it back, don't worry.' Tubbs picked up the note, slipped it into his pocket, looked at his empty glass. 'Don't mind if I have a nightcap.' He calmly opened the cupboard, took the whisky bottle, poured from it. There was a faint click. 'Hallo, hallo, what have we here?' The compartment door had opened. Tubbs held the wig in his hand.

'*What* have we here?' Tubbs repeated. He looked at the wig, smelt it, then pointed like a terrier, staring at the bald head opposite him. He came towards Arthur, shuffling his feet a little, the wig hanging from his hand. Arthur stayed still as Tubbs deftly placed the wig on his head, then chuckled and stepped back. His eyes stood out, the balls of them a dirty white. The tip of his tongue came out, washed round his mouth, went back.

Arthur snatched off the wig, threw it on to the table. Tubbs stared at him, raised the glass to his lips, sipped, put it down. 'I think I'll stay the night.'

'You will not.' He was surprised to hear his own voice so mild.

'We've got things to talk about. Explanations. You said so yourself.'

'I'll drive you to the station. Now.'

'I like it here. Country air. Good for the old ticker.' He placed his hand on his heart.

Arthur ran into the hall, picked up a loaded walking stick he kept there, came back. 'Get out. At once.'

Tubbs did not look alarmed. 'You don't mean that, you don't want me to go.'

'I do, I do.' He was not sure of the truth of his words. He advanced, holding the stick threateningly, loaded end pointed at Tubbs.

'You're being silly, old man. And you look silly too.'

Arthur struck at him across the table, a wild blow that missed completely, hit the table and chipped off a large splinter of wood.

'Steady on.' Tubbs snatched up the wig and moved round the table with it. Another blow struck his arm and caused a yelp of pain, but he did not drop the wig. Arthur suddenly reversed—it was like a sinister game of musical chairs—and stretched out a hand. Tubbs wriggled away from him, laughed, skidded round the end of the table, slipped and fell to the floor. Arthur pounced, grabbed the wig, stood over the prostrate man holding the stick menacingly, told him to get up. Tubbs did not move. Arthur prodded him with the stick, half-rolled him over. There was blood on his forehead. Where had it come from? Arthur knelt down and with a feeling of repugnance lifted the inert head. The blood came from the back of it. 'Tubbs,' he cried out. 'Stop play acting, Tubbs.' He let go of the head and it dropped to the floor. Obviously Tubbs had been taught a lesson. There was blood on the wood block floor which annoyed him. He brought in a damp cloth from the kitchen, wiped it up, gave the inert figure another prod. Two or three minutes passed before it occurred to him that Tubbs might be dead, and another two or three before he confirmed this with a small mirror put to the lips. Even then he did not truly believe it, searching desperately for a heart-beat and putting the glass again to the mauvish lips before acknowledging the truth. Among all the lies that Tubbs had told him there must have been one decisive fragment of truth. He really did have a weak heart. He had slipped, caught his head against the corner of the table, and been killed by the shock. Or perhaps he had a very thin skull, the exact cause of death did not seem important. What was he going to do about it?

In extreme situations action is for many people a kind of solace, and the logical reasoning that prompts it may be deliberately avoided. He could not have given reasons for his actions in the next hour, but if he could have formulated them they would have been that somebody in his position did not call the police. For such a tragedy to occur in the house of a man whose wife had so recently been murdered must arouse comment and investigation. And then think of the questions, who was Tubbs, why was he in the house, what was the connection between them? Once admit to knowledge of Tubbs and the police might go on to discover the swindle practised on him, find the solicitor who drew up the agreement, ask where the money had come from—there would be no end to it. The police had believed in Easonby Mellon because Arthur Brownjohn remained untouched by suspicion. Once cast a doubt upon him, and investigations would be made. But nobody knew that Tubbs had been in his house, and by his own account he had no dependants and no permanent lodging. If Clennery Tubbs disappeared there was nothing to connect him with Arthur Brownjohn.

He did not think like this, he did not think consecutively at all, while he acted. He opened the fibre suitcase and found in it a change of clothing, shaving things, a set of rigged cards for playing 'Find the Lady,' and some pornographic postcards. He put a couple of brown sacks that had been in the garage when he bought the house into the boot of the car, picked up the thing that had been Clennery Tubbs, half-dragged and half-carried it to the car and put it on top of the sacks. There passed through his mind the recollection of an

217

American case in which a woman, after killing her husband, had disposed of him over a bridge by tying heavy weights to his feet and hands and then tipping him over. It had been important to her that the body should not be discovered, but for him this did not matter because nothing connected him with it. He put the fibre suitcase into the boot and drove out into the night. The time was half past ten.

His road lay through small villages lying under the downs, Westmeston and Plumpton. He turned on to the main Lewes road at Offham, skirted the town, and drove down through Ilford and the tiny hamlet of Rodmell which is strung out along the main road. The night was fine and there was little traffic. He had just passed Rodmell when a vehicle behind him flashed its light on and off and then sounded a single sharp toot on the horn. In a momentary panic he accelerated and took a bend on the wrong side of the road. The toot was repeated. A motor-cycle passed, and cut in front of him. A hand waved. He stopped the car, wound down his window. The night was black and still.

The head that appeared was large. A policeman's helmet topped it. 'Take a bit o' stopping, don't you? Good job there wasn't a car coming round that corner. Bad bit of driving.'

'I'm sorry. I thought—' What could he say?

'Thought I was one o' those young

tearaways, did you?' A flashlight appeared. 'Could I see your driving licence?' The light played on the licence, then on his face. 'Thank you, sir. Did you know you were driving with only one rear light?'

So that was all! Gratefully, almost eagerly, he got out of the car, walked round to the back and tut-tutted. 'I'll have it seen to. Thank you very much.'

'Can be deceptive. Might think you're a motor-bike.'

'Of course, yes. I assure you it was perfectly all right yesterday.'

'Faulty connection may be. Or the lamp gone.' The policeman put his hand down to the boot and before Arthur could complete his agonised restraining gesture gave it a sharp blow with his clenched fist. The rear light came on. 'There you are, faulty connection. Bit of brute force, that's all you needed. Want to get it looked at, though.'

'Thank you very much. I will.' He began to move towards the driver's seat. The policeman, large and black in the black night, blocked his way.

'Tell you something else. I believe you've got a puncture. Back tyre, nearside.'

'Oh, I don't think—' But the policeman was already there, flashlight in one hand, tyre gauge in the other. Arthur took the flashlight and aimed it down at the stooped figure while the gauge was inserted. The policeman straightened up. His face was round and young.

'Down to twelve pounds. Slow puncture. Better change that tyre.'

'Yes.' The spare tyre in the Triumph is kept in the boot, beneath the luggage, together with the jack.

'I'll give you a hand.' The policeman repossessed himself of the flashlight.

He took a deep breath. 'Look, officer, I'm in a desperate hurry, my wife's ill, and I've only got a mile or two to go. This should last out till I get home and I'll change it then.'

The light moved from the boot to his face, back again, was switched off. 'Reckon so. Sure I can't help?'

'It's very kind of you, but I can get home.'

'Right then. Get that rear light seen to, sir, won't you?' He moved away, kicked the motor-cycle into action and was gone along the Newhaven road, leaving the night still again. Arthur leaned against the car. A spasm of nausea bent him double, then passed. When he began to drive again he felt as if he had suffered some physical attack. At the sign that said *Southease* he turned left past the church, down a narrow road. In less than five minutes he was at Southease Bridge.

There were other bridges in the district, but most of those that crossed fast-flowing rivers, like the bridge at Exceat, were on main roads. Southease Bridge, however, was on a tiny side road joining the main Lewes-Newhaven road from which he had come and a minor road winding from the coast up to the downs through the villages of South Heighton and Tarring Neville, to pass a cement works and rejoin another main road out of Lewes at the hamlet of Beddingham. The side road is little used even in the daytime and the wooden bridge is not constructed for heavy traffic. Beneath it the Ouse flows swiftly down to Newhaven and the sea. He tucked the car in off the road beside the bridge and turned off the lights. A sign beside the point at which he had stopped said: 'Southease Bridge. Maximum Safe 2 tons, including weight of vehicle.' There were chalk deposits opposite. He had no flashlight, but he did not need one. He took the suitcase from the boot, walked to the middle of the bridge, dropped it over and heard a splash. Then he put his arm round the body, lifted. It did not move. He pulled at it in panic, felt resistance, pulled again. The strength to lift seemed to have gone out of his arms. He dragged the thing along the road up to the bridge and along its planks. A last effort was needed, and he made it. He lifted, levered. Another splash and it was gone.

With a sensation of total disbelief he heard a vehicle coming towards him from the Tarring Neville road.

He had no time to think, no time even to get back into the car. He ran off the bridge and stood with his back to the road in the attitude of a man relieving himself, as a lorry moved on to the bridge and clattered slowly across. Headlights blazed, he seemed to feel the heat of them on his back. The bridge was so narrow that the lorry almost touched him, and for a moment he feared that it would stop. Then it moved on up to Rodmell, leaving only a tail light which vanished as it turned a curve. He was safe. He got back into the car and drove home by way of Beddingham. He did not change the tyre, and by the time he limped back into the garage it was almost flat.

On the following morning he put the sacks, which were spotted with blood, together with the wig, into the garden incinerator. In the afternoon he had the puncture mended at his local garage. There was no trace left that Clennery Tubbs had paid him a visit.

The disastrous excursion to Brighton had cured him of the desire to discover his true nature by contact with other people. One fine October morning he looked up at the green slope behind the house, seemed to see himself rolling down it as a child and his mother in her floppy hat above, and realised that he wished to paint. Why had he not thought of it before? At school he had painted with enjoyment. Perhaps he had always wished to paint, perhaps Clare's visits to her art class had involved an unconscious rivalry with him instead of with his mother. He bought an easel and paints and in the mild October days went out and painted the countryside round Plumpton and Ditchling. At first he put awkward blurs on to the paper, but within a week he was producing recognisable shapes, and as he compared his work with his mother's it seemed to him that he had a delicacy and exactness of touch which she had lacked. He felt also that he was truly emancipating himself for the first time from the feminine influences that had pressed on him throughout his life— his mother, Clare, Joan. He lived frugally, taking date and banana sandwiches on these expeditions and cooking omelettes at night. The sensation of peace was strong. When he met the Brodzkys one day he greeted them smilingly, but they ignored him. This might have upset him in the past, but it did so no longer. He had been living in this way contentedly for two weeks when he returned from a day's painting to find Inspector Coverdale's black Humber in front of his gate.

CHAPTER EIGHT

LAST CONVERSATION WITH COVERDALE

It was Sergeant Amies, as Coverdale generously admitted, who made the vital discovery in the case, although neither man fully realised its significance at the time. Amies had become really rather obsessed by the affair, and had taken to brooding over the files of statements and documents when he had a spare half-hour. One day he came in with one of the documents and said: 'Just take a look at that, sir. What do you make of it?'

Coverdale looked and made nothing of what Amies showed him, except that it was certainly odd. 'There must be some simple explanation.'

'Nice to know what it was though, eh, sir?'

Coverdale sighed. The case had hardly been a triumph, although he was not inclined to attribute the negative result to his own handling of the investigation. With retirement looming ahead his chief desire was to forget about it. 'A minor point. It's difficult to see what bearing it can have.'

'It may be a minor point, but it's a discrepancy.'

'Yes. Well. I don't feel we should use a day of our time to clear up a discrepancy of that sort.'

Amies's silence showed disagreement, and indeed Coverdale had the prickly feeling in his fingers that he associated with something left undone. He was not sorry when Amies reopened the matter by coming to him one day and saying: 'What do you think of *that*, sir?'

That was a report from the Sussex police

that a body, so far unidentified, had been found by some boys in the River Ouse near to its mouth at Newhaven. The body was that of a man about five feet seven inches in height, and he was already dead when he entered the water. Death appeared to have been caused by a blow on the head delivered with some severity, which had caused a skull fracture. He had been in the water for about a week and would not be easily recognisable. He was fully dressed in cheap clothing, with the exception of the fact that he was wearing only one shoe. There was no clue to his identity in his pockets. A cheap suitcase which had been found a couple of miles farther up the river might possibly be connected with him, but in any case its contents were of no help in tracing him. He was fairly well nourished, about forty years of age, with brownish sandy hair and beard, no distinguishing marks. A shoe which appeared to be the fellow to the one he was wearing had been found on the ground just beside a place called Southease Bridge, so there was a strong presumption that he had been thrown into the river at that point.

Coverdale read it and said: 'Well?'

'I've been in touch with Sussex and made a few inquiries. There's another little report here.'

The little report was from P.C. Robertson of the Sussex constabulary, to the effect that on the 30 September he had stopped a Triumph car number 663 ABC near Rodmell on the Lewes-Newhaven road, because it lacked a rear light. The car also had a slow puncture. The driver had seemed agitated and had refused P.C. Robertson's offer to help him change the tyre, saying that he only had a mile or so to go to see his wife, who was ill. His driving licence bore the name of Arthur Brownjohn. P.C. Robertson had returned to Newhaven and had seen no more of the car.

Coverdale tapped the paper. 'Why did Robertson report an incident like this?'

'I gather Sussex asked for reports of anything out of the way near the Ouse in the week before they found chummy. It meant nothing much to them but it does to us, wouldn't you agree, sir? I mean we know he hasn't got a wife for a start.'

'We certainly know that,' Coverdale said cautiously.

'And the bridge at this place Southease is only about a mile from Rodmell.'

'It's all a bit conjectural.'

'Yes, sir. I wonder, how would it be if I went down and had a look round for a day or two, see what I can dig up. In co-operation with Sussex, of course.'

So that was the way it was done. Amies in fact took a little more than a week, but the result fully justified it, and Coverdale went so far as to congratulate the Sergeant on the skill with which he had followed up the leads he

226

had discovered. It was time for action. Strictly speaking it was a Sussex affair since the body had been found in that county, but the circumstances were exceptional, and co-operation presented no problem. So it was Coverdale and Amies who walked to the garage as Arthur was putting in the Triumph.

He was carrying his easel and paints. He stopped when he saw them. 'You've got some news?'

'We may have, sir, and we may not,' Coverdale said heavily. 'We thought we'd stop by to have a chat.'

'I'm sorry if you've had to wait. If you'd let me know—' He opened the front door.

'Perfectly all right. We've been admiring the scenery. As a matter of fact the Sergeant here has spent the last few days in this part of the world.'

Brownjohn led the way into the living-room, where he put down his painting things. 'Very tidy,' Coverdale said approvingly. He looked at the pictures. 'Local scenes. Are they yours?'

'No. My mother painted them. Years ago. Will you have a drink?'

'Nothing to drink, thank you.' Both men sat down, Amies in a circular chair, the Inspector in one of modern design which suddenly tilted back, taking his legs off the ground. Brownjohn gave a giggle bitten off like a hiccup. Neither policeman laughed. Amies looked for somewhere to put his hat and placed it carefully on the floor, then took out note-book and pencil.

'So sorry, I should have warned you. About the chair I mean.' He went to a cupboard made in some light wood, opened it. They watched in silence while he poured whisky. 'Made this myself. Turning into a handyman. Inside compartment too.' He opened it to show them. 'Had a faulty catch, but I've put it right now.'

He sat down and sipped his whisky. His face and his bald head were shiny, his nostrils twitched. He looked like a rabbit, and about him there was as always the air of being slightly lost, unable to cope with the pace and roughness of life. It was not easy to imagine him hurting anybody.

A great deal might depend on the way in which the interrogation was conducted, the order in which things were said. Coverdale had discussed this at length with Amies, and they had settled both their tactics and their technique. With the most casual possible air, like a centre forward beginning a game of football by a pass tapped only inches to his inside left, Coverdale said: 'I wonder, do you know a man who goes by the name of Clennery Tubbs?'

It was a fine evening. Behind the two policemen little chips of white cloud scudded across a blue sky. Outside there was the garden, beyond the garden a road, a hill, freedom. Inside these walls was the force that threatened freedom. Arthur could feel it emanating from the lumpy Inspector and his sharp-nosed Sergeant. He knew that battle was being joined, and that his fate might depend upon the quickness of his reaction.

First move, time-wasting evasion. 'Has he something to do with my wife's death?'

'I didn't say that.'

A pause. Amies spoke. 'Clennery Tubbs, unusual name, you wouldn't forget it.'

'I was just trying to—your saying *goes by the name of*, you see, rather—let me think. Yes. I remember. I met him at a demonstration some months ago, when I was showing one of my inventions, a dish washer.' He was conscious of waffling. 'He tried to interest me in an invention of his own, a car cream. I looked into it, but it was no good. Why do you ask?'

'You haven't seen him recently?' A shake of the head. 'He was fished out of the river a few days ago.'

'I'm sorry. Though I can't say I cared for him.' Self-possession recovered.

'He was a bad boy,' Coverdale said. 'Went inside seven years ago for frauds on women. Prints on file, that's how we traced him.'

'Our information is that you saw him recently. Just before his death. Which took place on or about September 30th.' That was the Sergeant, sharpish.

'Met him?'

229

'Perhaps you'd like to tell us what you did on that day. Not so long ago. Just over two weeks.'

'I'll need to look at—I've got a calendar in my kitchen.' Amies went to the kitchen door and stood there while he stared at a calendar on the wall. Then he came back and they all sat down again. 'Of course. I should have remembered, I went to Brighton. Somebody told me about a club called the Robin Hood and I went in there and played roulette. I won some money. Then I left and came home.'

'You left?' Amies said. 'You were thrown out, weren't you?'

A flicker of alarm stirred in Arthur's stomach. They had traced his movements in Brighton.

'My information is that you attacked a Mrs. Hester Green, tore off and broke her necklace and had to be escorted out.'

'I had a little too much to drink.' He pushed away the whisky glass. 'I can't be quite sure about my movements afterwards.'

'I suggest that you met the man Tubbs.'

'No,' he said firmly. 'I'm quite sure I didn't.'

'Mrs. Green saw you talking to a man resembling him outside the club.'

Just as firmly he said, 'She's mistaken. Or telling lies.'

He felt the tension in the other men, and relaxed a little. They were guessing, they only had Hester's word for it that he had met

230

Tubbs, there could be no proof that he had visited the bungalow.

At the same time Coverdale, in his ridiculous tilting chair, knew that a trick had been lost. Amies should have phrased his questions differently, he had failed to maintain the pressure, they were not exactly back to square one but they would have to approach from a different angle. As Amies began to ask another question the Inspector cut him short.

'You agree that you attacked Mrs. Green?'

'Oh no, Inspector, of course not.' Brownjohn laughed, moved his chair nearer to the table in the middle of the room, rested his arm on it. 'I'd met her—I didn't even know that was her name—earlier in the day in the antique shop she runs, and when I saw her again in the club it was natural to buy her a drink.' Amies tried to interrupt and Coverdale checked him, saying that they must let Mr. Brownjohn speak. 'I didn't attack her—what happened was that I lurched across the table because I'd had one too many, slipped and caught my hand in her necklace. It's true that she was angry, but I assure you it was an accident.'

'It's not important,' Coverdale said soothingly. 'And after that you can't remember driving home?'

'That's right. But I did.'

'You left the club at about nine o'clock, right, Amies?' The Sergeant nodded sulkily.

231

'Did you drive straight back?'

Arthur thought: you've telegraphed your punch, my dear Inspector. That damned policeman on the motorbike has reported seeing me. 'I just don't know. I know I got home, but I don't know the time.'

'Your car was seen near Rodmell, a few miles south of Lewes, by a policeman. He stopped you and talked to you, and you showed him your driving licence. You had a dud rear light. This was just before eleven o'clock. Two hours to get from Brighton to Rodmell, which isn't more than twelve miles. How, do you explain that?'

'I can't. I told you I had too much to drink. I just drove around, or at least I suppose so. I do have a vague recollection of talking to a policeman.' He actually smiled and asked if they would like a drink now. He was pouring another for himself after they had shaken their heads when the Inspector said that if there was such a thing as a bottle of beer in the house, he did feel thirsty. As Arthur got up to fetch it he saw the surprised, almost hostile glance that Amies gave his superior, and thought: *I've convinced the Inspector, he's on my side now, I just have this surly brute to deal with.* Amies said: 'He was thrown into the river at Southease Bridge, not far from where the policeman stopped you.'

He did not falter in pouring the beer, but he thought: how can they know that? The

Sergeant provided the answer, in his voice that sounded like chalk on a blackboard. 'You wonder how we know? Because one of his shoes was left beside the bridge, that's why.'

The tug I felt when I got him out of the car, he thought. Amies went on.

'You were seen on the bridge. By a lorry driver. You'd just thrown the body over.'

He felt mildly contemptuous. Really, the man's *modus operandi* was crude. 'That isn't true.'

'If you were so drunk, how do you know? If you were drunk, why didn't PC Robertson notice it?'

He shrugged and decided that it was time to move on to the attack. 'I think you'll agree that I've answered your questions patiently, but now I'm going to refuse to say anything more until you tell me why you're asking them.'

A short silence. Then Coverdale. 'All right, sir. Tubbs was thrown into the river. He was dead when he went in.' Another silence. Should he comment? Better not. 'He had a slight heart condition, but the cause of his death was a blow on the head which fractured his skull.'

'A blow on the head.' He wanted to say that Tubbs had hit his head against the table, but of course that wouldn't do.

'Might have been from your stick.' That was Amies, who now fetched the stick from the hall, thwacked his palm with the loaded end,

233

nodded.

Indignation came up like bile. 'How did you know my stick was there? You've been inside this house. Illegal entry.'

'I happened to notice it as we came in.' Amies laughed in his face as he spoke, unpleasant. 'Handy weapon.'

'Outrageous,' he said. 'Outrageous.'

Coverdale finished his beer and said pacifically: 'Let's not get heated. Cards on the table is my motto. Your car was stopped a mile away from where Tubbs went into the river, it was identified by a lorry driver beside the actual bridge.'

'He was mistaken.'

'I'll be frank. What he saw was a figure near the bridge and a Triumph Herald car. He didn't get the number. Cards on the table. We were justified in asking questions, don't you agree?'

'And I've answered them.' Clouds were rolling up the sky, darkness softened the outlines of the room. The two figures sat like squat bugs in their chairs. He rose, turned on a standard lamp, drew the curtains across the windows, looked at his watch. 'If there's nothing more—'

'Just another couple of questions,' Coverdale said apologetically. 'About Mellon.'

'You've caught him?'

'I doubt we shall ever catch him now,' Coverdale said with a glance of meaningful directness. 'But the first question is this. Did you ever meet Easonby Mellon?'

'Certainly not.'

'Absolutely no question of it? You got that, Sergeant?' Amies had been making notes, and now made another. 'I want a positive answer, Brownjohn.'

'I've given it, haven't I? Damn you, how many more times?'

'Then how do you explain this?' A letter was thumped down on the table. He bent over it, unable at first to see anything more than the signature, 'Arthur Brownjohn' on the Lektreks paper. He began to read: 'I have known Major Mellon for several years, and it is my opinion that he will prove a reliable and respectable tenant . . .' It was the letter he had written long ago to the owners of the Romany House block as a reference. Who would have imagined that it still existed or that it would have come into the hands of the police? When he looked up his face was stricken.

'Credit where credit's due,' Coverdale said. 'Sergeant Amies spotted this.'

Amies had got up. 'Come on. Explain it.' They were both standing, one on either side of him. If ever a man looked guilty, the Sergeant said later to the Inspector, this wretched little figure looked guilty then. They asked questions in turn, so that his head moved first this way and then that, Coverdale's voice confiding, Amies's creaking with an occasional shrillness as if the teeth of a saw were being run over metal.

'On your firm's paper.'

'And your signature. We've had handwriting experts on the job.'

'So when did you first meet him? In the army?'

'No point in holding back any longer.'

'If you feel like making a statement now.'

'Make us do it the hard way and we'll be hard too. You wouldn't like it. How much did you pay him?'

The little man surprised them then. He got up, pushed past them, took one of the paintings off the wall (a hill, clouds, a house or two, they all looked much the same) and began to stamp on it. He burst into tears, his face contorted like a child's and suddenly grotesquely red. 'Lies, lies,' he cried out. 'The world's not like that, it's filthy.' He got his heel on to the pretty little picture and screwed it round. Coverdale, no art lover, felt quite upset. They stopped him as he was reaching for another picture. 'Steady on, now.'

Amies was not to be moved. He poked a bony finger into Brownjohn's chest. 'How much did you pay him?'

'Lies, all lies.' The voice was a scream. 'I don't know what you're talking about.'

'Sit down.' They had to push him into the chair. Coverdale said: 'Begin at the beginning. This letter. It was typed on your office

machine. Your letterhead. Your signature.'
Coverdale felt—well, hardly nonplussed but a
little taken aback—when Brownjohn denied
all knowledge of the letter. A simple denial is
often the most effective defence an accused
man can make in the face of what may seem
overwhelming facts. Here the facts were
powerful enough, but the man's admission of
them would be extremely helpful. Instead he
sat there blubbering and refusing to admit the
obvious. Now he had put his head on his arms
and was saying something unintelligible.

'What was that?'

'Go away. I'm not going to talk any more.'
Just like a small child.

'Just as I said, sir, we'll have to take him
along. No use doing it here.'

He looked up, showing a little tear-stained
red face. 'Along?'

'To the station. To help us with our
inquiries.'

'No.'

'It's no use getting into a tantrum.' With one
hand Amies began to pull him up from the
table.

'Stop it. You've got nothing against me.
What do you want me *for*?'

Coverdale put his lumpy face close to
Brownjohn's tear-stained one. 'I'm going to
tell you what happened. I'll tell you our
conclusions, and the evidence they're based
on. Cards on the table. When you've heard us

you can decide whether you want to make a statement or not. Fair enough?' Brownjohn sniffed, found a handkerchief and blew his nose.

'First of all, you wanted to get rid of your wife. You were too cowardly and too careful to do it yourself. So you hired a man to do it, a man you knew named Easonby Mellon. He ran a shady matrimonial agency, and the proof you knew about it is the reference you gave him. The idea, a clever one I admit, was that Mellon should write some letters pretending to have a love affair with your wife. You paid him to kill her.'

Brownjohn's fingers moved to his bald scalp, caressed it. 'That hotel in Weybridge—you told me Clare was there with him.'

'Mellon was there, but not with your wife. The woman with him wore a veil, but we've shown the hotel clerk pictures of your wife and he's sure that the woman at the hotel was a good deal younger. And we've never been able to find any other occasion when they met. Funny that, don't you think? Looks like a put-up job.' He waited for a comment but none came. 'Now, Sergeant Amies has been doing quite a bit of work on your affairs. You drew out five hundred pounds from your joint account in March—you drew it, not your wife. Why?'

'I—' Brownjohn fluttered his hands ineffectually. 'It was for Tubbs. For his invention. The car cream.'

'But you said you had nothing to do with that, you said it was no good.'

'It *was* no good, but I put some money in it. I was stupid. I bought—bought a share of the cream, I paid him the money, a solicitor named Eversholt drew up the agreement.'

Coverdale nodded, and Amies nodded in time with him. 'Now we're getting somewhere. You may be surprised to know that Sergeant Amies has talked to Eversholt.'

Amies took it up. 'He said the whole idea was so obviously potty he couldn't understand anyone with any sense putting money in it. He told you something to that effect, I believe.' Brownjohn fluttered his hands again. 'It was a cover, wasn't it?'

'I don't know what you mean.'

'When anyone asked why you'd paid out the money you'd tell them this story. It was a cover for the murder money, right?'

'I don't understand.'

'Then I'll tell you.' Amies thrust his razor nose within six inches of Brownjohn's rabbity one. 'Tubbs *was* Easonby Mellon.'

Brownjohn began to laugh. He stopped and then started again upon a higher note. Amies brought his hand round in a semi-circle. There was a sharp crack as it struck Brownjohn's cheek. The laughter stopped. Brownjohn put a hand to his cheek, nursed it. His reproachful eyes went from one of them to the other.

'The Sergeant had to do that, he didn't want to,' Coverdale said gently. The wounded eyes looked at Amies, who appeared ready to repeat the slap. 'And let's be frank about this, there's no proof of what we're saying. We know it's true, mind you, because of what happened afterwards, but there are no pictures of Mellon, and the only ones we've got of Tubbs are the prison pictures. So Eversholt can't help, and though we've shown the shots to people where Mellon had his office the results—I'm being frank—are inconclusive. Of course they're old pictures. We've got no positive identification. This is conjecture.'

'But it's impossible.'

Brownjohn looked as if he were about to giggle again, stopped when Amies asked sharply: 'Why?'

'We don't have any doubt that Mellon killed your wife, but we can't prove that you were an accessory. Can we, Sergeant?' Amies muttered something, got up from his chair and rubbed his bottom. 'But what we can prove is that you knew Mellon years before your wife's death, knew him well enough to give him a reference. And that he visited you here.'

'That he *what*?' Brownjohn took his hand away from his cheek. 'You must be mad.'

'The evidence, Sergeant.'

'Couple named Brodzky, live just up the road. They were walking past one evening—not September 30th, a few days earlier—and

240

saw this man in the garden. Very good description they gave, brownish or reddish hair, beard, ginger tweed suit. They realised who it might be at the time, being interested in the case, and they made a report to the local police.'

Coverdale coughed. 'Unfortunately it was ignored.'

'They were mistaken.'

'Oh no, they weren't. Mellon, or Tubbs whichever you like to call him, was here. You disposed of his clothes, didn't you, got rid of that ginger suit. Or you thought you'd got rid of it. You've got the doings in your brief-case outside, Sergeant, haven't you?'

While Amies was out of the room Arthur stared at the face of the Inspector as if he were examining the physical features of some unknown country which held the secret of his fate. Below thick dark-silvery hair a low forehead and then that worn knobbly face with its shallow bloodshot eyes, cheeks and chin full of unexpected promontories, the whole a mottled red in colour and bordered by a pair of ears so incongruously small, neat and pale that they might have been made of wax. Was it possible that this coarse and clumsy figure—the body below such a face would be clumsy, the feet certainly clodhoppers—could be in charge of his future? When he tried to move his left leg he was alarmed to feel that it was paralysed. He had the sensation, common to

241

those who have lost a limb, of making an attempt at movement and at the same time being aware of its impossibility. He bent down so that he could look under the table. His leg was moving when he gave it instructions! It moved quite definitely, made a little twirl in the air, twitched as though a jumping bean were inside it. Why did he feel that it was not moving at all, why was it dissociated from him?

'The Sergeant took a bit of a liberty. While you were out on your painting expeditions I mean.' That was Coverdale, his mouth opening and closing like a dummy's. He did not hear the next words properly because he was conscious of the fact that his leg was still moving although he had given it instructions to be still. He caught the last phrase: ' . . . in your incinerator.'

It startled him. 'What is that? What did you say?'

To his bewilderment they did not answer. Instead the Sergeant, with a smile like a shark's, drew something slowly out of a black brief-case. He watched fearfully until the thing was right out and then relaxed. It was only a sheet of paper! Then with a pounce Amies had put the thing in front of him and asked if he recognised it.

He stared at it, seeing a large photograph of what appeared to be some kind of medal, with a fragment of a flag (was it a flag?) adhering to it. He looked up questioningly.

242

'Come *on* now.' That was Amies, a nasty customer. 'Look at it, man, look.'

The thing he had taken for a medal was a button. There were letters on it and he spelt them out soundlessly. I-N-C-H-&-B-U. What did the ampersand mean? Then he looked up.

'I see you've got it. Corefinch and Burleigh. High class firm, they put their name on the fly buttons. And the material, recognise that? High class again, they knew the customer it was made for. Guess who? Easonby Mellon.'

'Fly buttons,' Coverdale said meditatively. 'Old-fashioned now, everyone wears zips, but they're old-fashioned tailors.'

'You know where it came from.' That was Amies, and it was not a question. *'Look at me.'*

He looked, at Amies's dead sallow face and Coverdale's bumpy one, and saw no help in them. Then he glanced down. Below the table his leg kept up its jigging without prompting from him. He put a hand to his face and felt nothing, although he knew that finger must have touched cheek.

Amies had his hand in the brief-case again. Another photograph was put in front of him. He turned his face away and refused to look, until Amies raised a menacing fist like a parent threatening a child. Then he did not understand what he saw.

'Bit of sacking,' the Sergeant said. 'From the incinerator. Careless you were, just a few inches not burned, but enough. Stain on it—

there—look.' He did not look. 'Marvellous what the boys can do now. They say it's blood, group AB, very unusual. Know what Tubbs's blood group was? AB.'

Sacking, sacking? He remembered the sacking in the car, but it belonged to another time. He glanced down again. His leg had stopped twitching, his limbs were dead.

'Let's recapitulate,' Coverdale said. 'We believe you hired Mellon to kill your wife and that afterwards he tried to blackmail you. We believe that, but we can't prove it. This is what we can prove. You knew Mellon years before your wife's death, and you lied about it. You paid Mellon or Tubbs, whichever you like to call him, money for a completely useless invention. Mellon came here to see you— we've got witnesses to that. You were seen to meet him in Brighton on the night of September 30th. You burned the clothes Mellon was known to wear in your incinerator, and you burned the sacking with bloodstains that are the same blood group as Tubbs's on it. Your car was positively identified a mile from where Tubbs went into the river, and almost as positively identified at the very bridge. Mellon and Tubbs have both been here, we can prove it. There's a strong presumption they were the same person. If you say they're not, you've got to answer one question. *Where is Easonby Mellon?*'

The Sergeant echoed the question, and he

244

knew he could not answer it. Beyond Amies, directly behind his head, was one of the little thin paintings on the wall, but it gave him no help. There was no way out.

He opened his mouth. 'I—' He was unable to go on. He felt the paralysis creeping up his body.

'I think he's ready to make a statement now, sir.'

His hand clasped his throat, plucked at it to release the words that at last came up. 'I killed Easonby Mellon.'

Coverdale let out breath in a sigh and said gently, 'Come along with us.' They lifted him, but when they tried to stand him up he slipped sideways like a rag doll. In the end they had almost to carry him out to the car. He appeared to have lost the use of his legs.

*   *   *

Arthur Brownjohn did not stand trial. He was found unfit to plead under the McNaughten Rules on insanity and this, as Coverdale said to Amies, was just as well, because the medical evidence about the blow and some of the other evidence too was distinctly shaky. The temporary hysterical paralysis he had suffered from soon passed away, and in Broadmoor he was a quiet tractable inmate who spent a great deal of time in painting. Most of his paintings were water colours of imaginary Sussex landscapes, and some of them were displayed in prisoners' art shows. His work in oils, however, was quite different. It depicted scenes in which a lusty naked man with thick hair and curling beard, rather like a Rubens satyr, stabbed or strangled a naked woman who limply submitted to her fate. These pictures obviously excited him considerably, and they interested the doctors, but they were not thought suitable for exhibition. As time passed he painted fewer of them, and at length he stopped asking for oil paints. He ate voraciously, grew fat and seemed quite happy.

We hope you have enjoyed this Large Print book. Other Chivers Press or G.K. Hall & Co. Large Print books are available at your library or directly from the publishers.

For more information about current and forthcoming titles, please call or write, without obligation, to:

Chivers Press Limited
Windsor Bridge Road
Bath BA2 3AX
England
Tel. (01225) 335336

OR

G.K. Hall & Co.
P.O. Box 159
Thorndike, Maine 04986
USA
Tel. (800) 223-2336

All our Large Print titles are designed for easy reading, and all our books are made to last.